PERFECTLY PRETTY
& other love stories

Johanna Miklós

PERFECTLY PRETTY
& other love stories

Copyright © 2014 by Johanna Miklós

ISBN 0990636003
ISBN 978-0-9906360-0-7

Cover design by Simona Doxan

Acknowledgments

I would like to thank my editors Russell Bittner, Helga Schier of With Pen and Paper, and Amy Maddox of The Blue Pencil for their invaluable contributions; Simona Doxan for cover design; and my family and partner for their unconditional support.

Table of Contents

Perfectly Pretty   1

Breadcrumbs   21

Eugene & Kuki   71

Magariah's Flaw   123

Ophelia Rekindled   145

Perfectly Pretty

My darling, darling Sara-Beth,

She who HAS NO RIGHT TO TELL YOU HOW TO LIVE YOUR LIFE has something to tell you.

This morning, She woke at her usual hour. Like every morning since the day you were born, her thoughts went to you. She wanted to jump out of bed, wake you, get breakfast going, get you ready for school, get herself to work—and then She remembered that you have gone to live with your boyfriend. So She stretched,

1

rotated her wrists, and was about to pedal her feet to get the old circulation going when She heard a soft snore.

Yes, my darling. She who KNOWS NOTHING ABOUT MEN, She who HATES ALL MEN since your father dumped her for a Vegas show girl, had a MAN in her bed. She also remembered the previous night's events. (She will spare you the details; after all, She is your mother.) Anyway, She jumped out of bed, ran to the bathroom, and locked the door. She needed a little time to think things through. There is nothing like a warm bath for thinking things through. As you may remember, She wanted a tub—this would have been the perfect time for a long soak—but the shower you insisted on had to suffice.

Once under the warm spray, She found herself wishing the stranger in her bed would take the sponge and spread foaming body wash all over her back and hips. She let herself imagine a gentle shoulder massage, murmured compliments, and his strong fingers exploring her wet body. She who IS AN OLD PRUDE writes these intimate thoughts not to shock you, my darling, but to let you know She is not just your mother, and a business owner, but also a woman.

Then, She admits here, She felt foolish and decided to end it right there. She stepped out of the shower, covered herself in the bulky, terry cloth robe you gave her for Christmas, and marched back into the bedroom.

Clutching a pillow to his chest, the stranger was still fast asleep. She was torn—wake him up and throw him out? Join him under the covers? Finally, She who ALWAYS KNOWS BEST did neither.

3

She took her clothes, shoes, and purse to the living room and dressed there. And then She who IS NEVER AT A LOSS FOR WORDS stared blankly at the notepad by the phone. She didn't know what to say to this stranger in her bed.

During the drive to work, She wondered whether She had lost her mind. You, my darling, may be thinking the same thing! We both know She is not "that kind of woman."

She went to Avery's—as She does every morning—to have a hot bun and a coffee. She hoped you would stop there on your way to school. But no. Christy came, though, and also had a coffee. By the way, Christy never eats a bun—that's how she keeps her figure. This is not a continued CRITICISM OF YOUR EATING HABITS, my darling, just facts. She is giving Christy great credit here for tact: no mention of you at all. Not a word about the SCENE you caused yesterday. Christy asked instead if She is going to hire Matty, the girl from Oregon. You didn't meet the young woman—she came by yesterday after your BLOWUP and asked if the store had any openings. Christy said Matty could do with a makeover. "The pioneer look doesn't go with the image of Perfectly Pretty beauty salon." There was something wholesome about Matty. Or maybe there was something sad. Whatever it was, it wasn't artificial. But Christy is right; the clients expect the employees to look glamorous.

She opened the salon and, with Christy's help, got through the busy morning. You, my darling, didn't call. She who loves you with all her JUDGEMENTAL heart also has her pride and resisted the temptation to call you.

5

Matty also didn't show. Instead, this skinny guy came. He slouched at the register talking to Christy, who really had no time to chat. She who THINKS SHE CAN TELL EVERYTHING ABOUT EVERY-BODY BY JUST LOOKING AT THEM didn't know it was Matty's lazy husband.

"The Oregon girl's going to be late," Christy said. "One of her four kids has to see a doctor, plus she needs her license approved." The guy didn't say anything, but his pointy Adam's apple was jumping up and down like a frog on drugs. He was swallowing his drool so fast and stripping Christy with his rheumy eyes. Blech! Why didn't he take the kid to the doctor? That's the worst kind, my darling. Nothing to do, no place to go, but won't help the wife. Ogling pretty, young things instead!

By noon, She was half convinced the night with the stranger never happened. And if it had, it was over. He would be gone and nobody would ever know—not even you, my darling daughter.

There was a lot of work. Luckily, Matty finally showed up with a provisional license and her hair in a nice updo. Clients just came streaming in, and everybody wanted the goldie streaks. There were only a few kits left, and She was hoping the promised delivery would arrive before all the kits were gone. She who MAKES EVERYBODY WORK OVER-TIME sent Christy and Matty home on the dot at six! She who MAKES OTHERS DO THE DIRTY WORK cleaned up alone, did the books, and waited in vain for the delivery until the mall closed. It was very late by then. You, my dear daughter, hadn't called all day. She who BELIEVES IN EDUCATION LIKE IT'S A MAGIC PILL hopes you went to school.

On the drive home, She wondered whether you would be there. She also wondered if the stranger would still be at the house. Then She worried. What if you had come home and met the man at the house? What would you think of your mother? She spent the drive preparing herself for all possible scenarios.

It was dark by the time She got home. There were no lights on in the house. She felt very sad as she sat alone in her car in the driveway and looked at the empty little house. Then She saw movement on the porch. She thought you had come home! She jumped out of the car and then saw it wasn't you. There he stood, as he had the night before in the Chinese restaurant: slightly stooped and holding an old, brown leather briefcase. He said he was just leaving and that he thought She had only gone out for coffee and that *he'd waited for her to come back ALL DAY*. She who NEVER MAKES A FOOL OF HERSELF forgot all the clever lines She had prepared and babbled about Avery's fabulous buns that are only good hot, traffic to Salt Lake that gets worse by the day, and mall security that carries guns since that kid shot all those people at Trolley Square. She who ISN'T AFRAID OF ANYTHING admitted She gets nervous when She sees someone in a hoodie.

He said he thought She just wanted him to disappear and wasn't coming home because She was afraid of running into him. Then She remembered their conversation the previous evening. They hadn't talked about work! She who is ALL WORK WORK WORK had discussed food, country music, movies, and line dancing. They had also talked about seaweed and mermaids for a reason She still can't recall. She finally told him She had gone to work in the morning and that She owns the Perfectly Pretty beauty parlor at the mall. He looked impressed. By then they were back in the house.

She who BORES you when she talks about work realized he wanted to hear all about it. She sat down in the living room with him and explained why she went with a franchise—the name recognition and all that.

Logan's cheeks dimpled—that's his name, by the way. It's a nice name, don't you think? His nose sort of crinkles when he smiles. She has to tell you, his smile is a very warm smile. It makes She who is ALWAYS COOL-HEADED feel quite light-headed. She obviously didn't tell him his smile was having that effect on her. She is, after all, your mother and not some naïve teenager.

Anyway, She told him all about the goldie streaks, and the kits from Perfectly Pretty, and that MORON Ochenbraun at Perfectly Pretty headquarters in Oregon who just won't send enough, and that now the store is totally out She didn't know what to tell the clients tomorrow. And then—because he was all smiles and playing with the strings on her pink and red sweater, and because you could still come through the door at any minute, and because it was just time to say everything—She told him all about the scandal you caused at the salon and your decision.

Right there, She let-the-cat-out-of-the-bag-dropped-the-bomb and aired the family laundry. She wanted him to know he was flirting with an abandoned and failed single mom! He just smiled and held up three fingers. Logan has three kids!

11

Can you believe it? Like She who's NEVER MADE A MISTAKE IN HER LIFE, he also had to get married right out of high school. His three are all grown and married, and now he's even a grandfather.

He said he looked for a note, and then he thought of writing a note, and then he knew that it was important for him to see "the woman with the perfect hair" again. She told him, "Perfect hair comes with the territory," and that made him laugh. She hasn't made you laugh in a long time, has She? She who NAGS ALL THE TIME thought about that, too.

Then he took a deep breath, and here is pretty much what he said: "I'm not married, Wendy. My wife and I divorced ten years ago after the kids were grown. I'm not a Romeo or a con artist. When I walked into that place"—he meant the Chinese diner—"I don't know what possessed me! I don't even like Chinese food. But I was tired, and it was next to the hotel where I'm staying. Anyway, I saw you. You're really pretty, Wendy. I knew in my gut, in my heart, and in my head: if I don't do something right now, that beautiful woman's going to finish her dinner and walk out."

Can you imagine? This man just fell for your mother head over heels.

She who is "not that kind of woman" said that She didn't know what possessed her to bring him home last night, and he said, "It felt right."

So he stayed and waited. Logan sat at the kitchen table all morning and slept on the sofa all afternoon, and then it grew dark and he decided he'd better go because it was late and the pretty woman (that's your mother!) wasn't coming back and he must have been delusional when he thought the magic was mutual.

She who ALWAYS USES WORK AS AN EXCUSE told him She waited until the mall closed for the kits from Oregon that Ochenbraun insisted were being delivered today. Otherwise, She would have been home sooner.

"This is just too stupid," Logan said then. "I could've known by your hair and the scent of Pretty Wild Spring conditioner. I just didn't think. That's the effect you have on me. We came here in your car last night, so you didn't see my Perfectly Pretty van. If you take me to my hotel, I'll be happy to give you all the streak kits you want."

She who is NEVER RUDE TO ANYONE thought She was sitting opposite "that moron Ochenbraun." It was a mortifying, ready-to-faint-with-embarrass-ment moment.

Thank goodness it wasn't quite that bad. It turns out Ochenbraun works for Logan. But it was actually Logan who was "the moron." Ochenbraun had put the kits in the van, and Logan was supposed to deliver them to the parlor before checking in to the hotel!

The short of it is, She who is JUST ANOTHER WORKER BEE is a pretty good worker bee. It seems her salon in Utah has been using more kits than any other franchise in the country, and Logan wanted to see for himself how this was possible.

So, my darling, here is what happened: She who DRIVES YOU CRAZY with her attention to detail explained how to apply the finest golden highlights instead of clumsy gashes of color like everybody else. Logan, a savvy business-man when he's not busy flirting, made an amazing offer: She will become a corporate trainer to all franchise owners and their staff in this special process. Plus, there will be instruction videos to shoot and booklets to print.

Logan is waiting for her to pack her bags. Next stop: Las Vegas. Also, he pro-posed. As he says, it feels right. She who NEVER DOES ANYTHING SPONTANEOUS agrees. And you, my stubborn daughter, can now say you have two parents who ran away to Vegas, albeit sixteen years apart.

Much love,

She, also known as MOM

Perfectly Pretty and other love stories

Johanna Miklós

Breadcrumbs

Johanna Miklós

Solange plucked little snowballs from her frayed, black leg warmers and lined them up on the stoop. "He loves me. He loves me not. He loves me. I love him not," she counted softly. If Virgil comes now, she thought, it's not over. If he's not in, she promised herself, I'll go home and never come back.

Virgil, a lumpy, gray duffel bag slung over one shoulder, opened the glass-paneled door of the squat student residence.

"Doing laundry," he said without smiling.

"I have to see you." Solange looked for warmth in his dark eyes.

Virgil hesitated and then stepped back to let her into the low-ceilinged, fluorescent-lit entrance. He closed the door. "I'll just check my mail."

Perfumed air rose from the dryers in the basement of the building, warmed Solange's cheeks, and melted the snow on her coat and hair while she waited for Virgil to return from the mailroom. The drops fell, first on the scuffed linoleum floor where they created a puddle, then in a trail on the concrete steps as she followed him up to his apartment.

Virgil pushed open the door and took his laundry straight through to his bedroom. The closed doors to the two other bedrooms and unusual silence let her know that his roommates were not there.

For the first time since they met, Solange did not follow him but stayed in the dark living room. She heard the click of the switch in his room. A sliver of light cut a path between the two rooms, its fallout casting the living room in shades of gray. She dropped her wet coat on the back of a chair, stepped over piles of books and sports gear to the metal-framed windows, and leaned her forehead against the cold glass. She looked through her own reflection at the outside world. A thick layer of snow coated leafless branches, benches, the lawn, and narrow paths of the park between the student residences.

"Ne pas toucher," she whispered. She wished for Do Not Touch signs, like those preserving museum treasures.

Solange looked without blinking until the plain white sheet fragmented into millions of intricately connected crystals; until a gust of wind blew a large flake to the window pane, its facets a jagged labyrinth, inviting her to touch and warning her to keep away; until Virgil strolled in.

The light cast shadows under his tapered chin and highlighted his high forehead, almond-shaped eyes, and narrow, straight nose. It had been the first thing she had noticed about him: the features she associated with icons in museums and on the walls of Russian Orthodox homes. Ideal, spiritual beauty— that's what she had thought when they first met. After nine months as his lover, she was still awed by his Byzantine face. Overwhelmed by desire, Solange rushed to him and crushed his sharply delineated mouth with her lips.

"Can't we rewrite the script?" she murmured after she released his mouth. Virgil shook his head and avoided her eyes, and Solange picked up her coat and headed for the door.

"Where are you going?" he asked.

"Away," Solange said softly as she choked back tears. She opened the door and blinked at the harsh fluorescent light in the stairway.

"You take one step down those stairs, and I'll never see you again!"

Solange laughed at the absurdity of his threat and the delight of the invitation. She closed the door again and followed him into the galley kitchen.

Virgil opened the scratched-up yellow refrigerator and waved at its contents. "Hungry?" On the shelf that bore his name, there was a half-eaten hamburger that sat between a blackened carton of cream cheese and some spotted apples. He grabbed the burger and bit into it.

"You sure that's safe to eat?" Solange drew back in disgust. Virgil spat the partly chewed food into the sink.

"I'm tired," he announced. He tugged the sweater over his head and dropped it at her feet. His naked shoulder brushed the tip of her nose as he edged past her out of the kitchen.

"Why are you making this so hard on us?" Virgil asked. Without waiting for an answer, he escaped into the bathroom.

Solange dropped her coat on top of his sweater and followed him. She heard the water from the shower and gave the closed bathroom door a feeble punch. "Because I can't stop myself."

Solange switched off the bedroom light and waited for him to finish his shower. She stood by the window in his messy room observing the dance of snowflakes under the cold glow of a street lamp.

"I can't talk now." He stretched out on the permanently unmade bed and buried his face in the pillow.

Solange felt the strain of loss, the pain she had grappled with and not overcome for the past two weeks since Virgil had ended their affair, and broke the barrier that protects the observer from the art. She crossed the room and sat down on the bed.

"I can't believe I'll forget how your skin feels." She traced the rivulets that snaked from his wet hair and met between his shoulder blades. She drew a line with her finger down his back to his slim waist and soft buttocks. "Why does there have to be a last time?"

Virgil groaned and turned over. He pulled Solange on top of himself on the narrow mattress and kissed her.

Solange's mind shut down as his tongue took over her mouth. All she sensed, all she lived for in that moment was his scent. She felt her own pulse in her lips as his pressed against them, their mouths joined in an endless, hungry kiss. She helped him pull off her clothing, every inch of her skin full of desire to touch his. Then she gave herself to his caressing hands. She pressed herself against his long, athletic body and explored his nakedness as if this were the first time they were making love. Then, when their bodies ached to be joined, she held his gaze and steered his hips. . . .

Her lust satisfied, Solange was instantly repelled by him and by what she had done. She tore her cracked, perspiring skin from his and sat up in the bed that had suddenly become too small for two people.

"This is what we can't talk about." Virgil's abandoned body shivered and he pulled the cover up from where it lay on the floor.

"What happens to us?"

"Out of control," he finally said.

"I feel afraid."

"I know." He put his arm awkwardly around her shoulders and pulled her back down beside him. "Let's just sleep together, Solange. We've never done that."

"I'm so miserable. I wish . . ." Solange felt his arm stiffen. She struggled against the weight of his arm, against the suffocating heat of his distressed body, and rolled off the bed and groped in the sparsely lit room for her scattered clothes.

"I can't marry you," he said from the bed where he now lay alone.

Solange covered her nakedness with the oversized sweater—warm to the touch, it brought back a memory of the moments before Virgil had pulled it up and over her head. "This is the eighties," she said. "We don't have to be married to make love."

"That's how I was raised," Virgil said and watched as she finished dressing. "It's what I should do. It's the right thing to do when a man and a woman get together and have sex. But I've got to finish school. I've got a plan, Solange. I've worked really hard to get where I am, and I won't throw all that . . ."

Solange hurried away from his monologue to the kitchen to get her coat.

"You're like a drug!" Virgil suddenly appeared and slammed her against the kitchen wall. "I don't want to need you!"

Then the door to his bedroom banged and Solange fled. She ran down the stairs and out onto the sidewalk, where sparkling snowflakes cooled her burning face. Over. It's finally over, and it doesn't even hurt, she told herself. She slipped on the ice and fell into a mound of snow. I have to get away, she thought as she stood up and shook snow from her hands. She walked slowly down the sidewalk into the alley that led to the park. There she was struck by the turmoil that suddenly erupted in her heart. How long had it been since she had stood at his window and stared down at this picture-book landscape? Minutes? An hour? The park was still the same: pristine and cold. Stark white and strong shadows. The only sound was the breath that left her in anguished gasps. Solange took a fistful of snow and stuffed it in her mouth to silence the howl she felt forming in her soul. She pressed her cold hands to her burning eyes and stood still until the waves of dizziness and nausea subsided, until the cold seeped through her shoes and skin and reached her bones. Then she gathered herself and walked, hunched and alone with knowledge of who she was, deeply shaken. Again, little white snowballs formed on the frayed ends of her leg warmers as she slowly climbed over shifting snow mounds.

***

Solange folded her lined kid gloves, slipped them into the pocket of her camel hair coat, and let it slide off her shoulders to cascade in rich folds from her perfumed elbows. Daniel eased the mink-trimmed sleeves over her small hands. She heard the soft swish of the silk scarf under the collar of his tweed jacket as he handed her coat to the maître d'.

"Love your outfit." He pecked her heavily powdered cheeks. "Snow queen. Even your face matches. That's great!"

A winter-white light wool dress draped her body, the soft folds of the skirt ending at her knees, and off-white opaque tights matched high heeled pumps. Solange placed a manicured hand lightly on Daniel's arm as he led her over a thick Oriental rug to the deep green leather couch by the fireplace.

"Looks more like Michigan than DC." Daniel pointed at the wall of snow pushing against French windows. "Only there it takes a lot more to keep everyone off the streets."

He ordered champagne and strawberries from a smiling waitress.

"Let's drink to absent patrons and your courage to wear heels in this weather!"

"To all that isn't real!" Solange added when the drinks arrived. It was her choice to meet at this inn where Daniel had taken her on their first date almost two years earlier. "I can't believe we're the only ones here! Does snow freeze romance?"

"Not for me. I'm glad you like this place as much as I do." He offered her a strawberry from the crystal bowl. "It's the perfect setting for you."

The fire warmed his rounded cheeks and gave a mischievous sparkle to his pale eyes.

"I like paintings and not photographs," Solange said. "Paintings are about eyes, photographs about mouths."

"Except Bette Davis," Daniel teased.

"You went to your gym."

"How can you tell?"

"Your scent." She remembered traces of it on her hands. "I checked all the drugstores in DC but couldn't find it. Must be something your club has specially blended." She flipped open her cigarette case. "What's the news you have to tell me?" she asked as Daniel struck a match and held the flame to the tip of her cigarette.

"I'm engaged." He watched her inhale and the widening of her eyes at his announcement.

Solange blew out a thin stream of smoke between her heavily painted lips. "Do I know her?"

"No." He tossed the match into the fireplace. "I met Alison at a party in New York last August. I saw this perfect woman standing by a window looking out at the skyline and I thought, I've got to meet this creature! And I did." He grinned and bit into a strawberry.

"Congratulations. Why did you keep her a secret?" Solange asked and managed a smile. "Worried that I'd be jealous? I told you about Virgil."

"Yes, I remember. We haven't seen much of each other since you met him. Are you still madly in love?"

"Yes," admitted Solange and contemplated the white wall of snow pressing in on their warm retreat. "I am but he's not. I'm leaving the States."

"Come to London," Daniel urged. "It's where we'll be living. Alison's British."

"I'll go home to my parents," Solange finalized her decision. "I miss Paris."

"And this man you're seeing?" asked Daniel. "What if he wants you to stay?"

Solange shook her head.

"When I saw you in the summer, you looked like a woman living the passion of her life!" Daniel reminded her. "I thought you accepted the internship to stay here because of him. You said it was serious."

"It is for me. But passion alone isn't enough." As soon as she said it, Solange realized that it was true. "I stopped at the 7-Eleven by my house to buy cigarettes on my way here. Virgil was at the counter pouring himself coffee. He said, 'Nice coat.' He didn't smile. He also said, 'You look great.' We talked as if we were just acquaintances. As if he was not the man who a few days ago slammed me against a wall. Like a casual acquaintance and not the lover who rejects me as an evil drug."

"To us!" Daniel raised his flute.

"Friends after having been lovers," said Solange and instantly regretted it.

37

Daniel looked surprised. "We've never talked about that."

"I know," Solange struggled to repair the damage. "We moved from one form of friendship to the next and back again without discussions, declarations, or recriminations. That's a good thing. I didn't mean it as criticism."

They had met in the first weeks after Solange arrived in DC as an exchange student from Paris. Daniel, a native of the area, took obvious pleasure in showing Solange Washington's insider spots—such as this inn. It had been after one of their dinners at the inn that they had found themselves in the park by the cathedral. Their need for each other that night demanded instant gratification, precluding any attempt to reach a more private place. What began as a passionate encounter had ended swiftly in mutual yet silent disappointment.

"I think Chekhov said friends only after having been lovers," Daniel shared his understanding of their relationship. "Perhaps he had a point."

"Do I want too much?" asked Solange, violating their tacit no-judgment pact.

"We never want too much love."

"I'll always love you." Solange observed his reaction to her declaration over the rim of her empty glass.

"Maybe I should marry you," Daniel said with a small smile. "But what we have isn't enough for you, is it?"

Tears formed in her eyes, and Daniel offered his hand.

"The other isn't either," Solange wrapped her fingers around his.

"You want to live extremes, dear." Daniel caught a tear with his thumb. "Infernal passion and fairy-tale romance, draft-dodging complicity and dragon-slaying heroism, poetic slumming and jet-set parties."

"I'm not Virginia Woolf or Simone de Beauvoir! You make me sound greedy and insane."

"Fascinating and brilliant ladies!" Daniel corrected her. "There's nothing wrong with being greedy, Solange. Modesty's a questionable virtue. It only keeps people in sad, gray places, leading uninspired lives. Modesty certainly does nothing for art, or progress, or me."

"What will I do without a friend who believes all that?" Solange laughed outright through her tears.

"I'll leave a trail of breadcrumbs," he promised.

***

Solange paced back and forth between open suitcases in her bedroom and a growing heap of clothes in the living room. She kicked the frayed jeans, threadbare shirts, shabby sweaters, cracked and worn shoes, and the old coat. She went back to the bedroom and picked up a long chain of fake pearls from her dresser. I wore these to bed one night and nothing else, she thought. Then she stopped her thoughts and said aloud, "I have to get away." She rolled the necklace into a ball and threw it from the bedroom in a high arc onto the scattered heap in the living room.

Solange wanted to tear up match books from restaurants they had not eaten in, playbills from shows they had not seen, love letters Virgil never wrote,

41

and goofy cards he had never sent. She longed to rip smiling photographs never taken. She craved breaking gifts never received.

"I have to get away!" Solange chanted more and more loudly to drown the ache for everything their relationship had not had, until she screamed, "I HAVE TO GET AWAY!"

She pounded what little evidence there was of them as a couple—the grungy secondhand clothes she wore only for him—into a heavy-duty garbage bag.

"What's special about smelly old clothes?" Solange had wondered when Virgil had criticized her fashionable clothes and suggested she shop at secondhand stores.

"You're pretending to be new when you're used," Virgil had explained. "I'm used so I wear used clothes. I buy used books. I accept the flawed man I am. I don't pretend to be something I'm not. I don't buy newness."

"But that's like wearing someone else's life," she had protested when she had tried on a torn pair of jeans. "It's like I'm wearing her skin cells and her smell. Someone lived a life in these. Maybe she did something horrible in them. Maybe something horrible happened to her. In new clothes, there's no history. I like that. I like that only my life is in them and on them."

"Were you a virgin?"

"Don't be silly," she had said and hoped the salesperson had not heard Virgil's question.

"Then dress as what you are." His eyes had been clear and bright with conviction, like those of a saint. "Used. We're both used. The clothes are like the lovers you had before me: strangers on your skin."

I have to get away. I have to get away. Solange aimed the mantra at her longing for Virgil. She hunted one more time through her closet, drawers, and nightstand. Then she made a solid knot in the plastic bag and carried her disguises, the only mementos of their relationship, to the back of the building and dumped them in a large garbage container.

***

A cramp spread across the left side of her face, tears streamed from her left eye, and her hands lay limp in her lap. Solange was in the grip of paralyzing pain caused by rapidly increasing altitude.

"Is this your first flight?" asked the Davidoff-aftershave-soaked man in the window seat.

Solange tried to shake her head and groaned at the effort. The over-scented man rang for the steward. Solange willed her breathing to remain even.

You look a fright, she interpreted the disgusted look on the face of the scotch-drinking passenger. She closed her eyes and escaped from the plane to the frozen sidewalk in front of the 7-Eleven.

She saw Virgil through a gap between posters announcing "Fresh Coffee Brewed 24/7" and "Breakfast Special for 99¢". He came out holding a cream-filled donut in his hands and stood so close that she could sense the rough texture of his army surplus coat.

"I haven't had a bite all day," he said instead of hello and bit into the pastry. "Let's walk."

The six o'clock news aired on the radio of a truck parked in front of the 7-

Eleven. The crime rate in DC was back to normal, schools would reopen the next day, and there was no more snow in the forecast.

He finished his sweet meal as they walked along the cleared sidewalk and then through the alley to the park behind the student dormitories. Neither one of them spoke. There were deep brown scars in the perfect white skin that had covered the muddy field for a few days. Children had used the past days off from school to build snowmen. They had even stripped the down-like covers from park benches and parked cars in their insatiable need for modeling material. Now a group of young men and women demolished the twig-nosed sculptures. They needed the snow for a friendly battle. "It's guys against girls!" they invited Virgil and Solange to join in.

"Forgot my gloves." Virgil held up his bare hands.

The wind carried frozen flakes from rooftops and branches in an illusion of renewed snowfall. Solange watched flakes alight on Virgil's ears and nose and listened to the crunch of his steel-toed boots crush the thin layer of ice on the path. She slipped and grabbed Virgil's arm to steady herself.

"Not practical," said Virgil about her high-heeled boots, but he let her cling to him until they were back at the 7-Eleven again.

"Want anything?" He was somewhere behind the rack of nuts and chips. Then he strode to the counter with a small box of chocolates and took a cellophane-wrapped rose from a blue plastic pail next to the chewing-gum and beef-jerky displays. He handed Solange the rose.

"Can I get you anything, Miss?" A hand touched Solange's shoulder. She opened a teary eye and recognized the airline uniform.

"A parachute."

"Aspirin!" ordered the perfumed, scotch-drinking man in the window seat.

Cyanide, Solange wanted to say as he leaned across her and opened the ventilation. His scent invaded her nose, his arm pushed against her tortured face, and Solange moaned in protest.

"Sorry." He leaned against her again to close the valve.

"Can you hold a cup?" asked the steward.

"I'll do that." The man took charge. "She'll just spill it. Open up. I'm putting a pill in your mouth and then some water."

She obediently parted her lips.

"Why don't you travel by boat?" he asked as he wiped her chin with a paper napkin.

"I get seasick," Solange tried to joke.

The aircraft reached cruising altitude, and the physical pain became tolerable. The man retreated to his headset and unfolded his newspaper. Solange closed her eyes again and drifted back to the snow-covered streets of DC.

"I have to finish packing," Solange finally told Virgil. "I'm leaving tomorrow."

He stuffed the chocolates into the pocket of her camel hair coat without a word.

"I'm going home," she said, although he had not asked where she was going or why. She watched him turn away and cross the street.

"Virgil!" she screamed and ran after him. "Wait!"

Virgil stopped in the middle of the deserted road.

"I heard you were leaving," he said. "I wondered if you were going to tell me."

"Promise me something," Solange begged, and she continued as she had with Daniel a day earlier, saying what she understood in the moment she said it. A truth, a synthesis of her emotions that suddenly presented itself in a clarity and with a finality that would remain with her for the rest of her life. One of those moments when we make a leap in maturity or experience, when our minds understand the summary of our experience before the heart can make peace with it. "Promise me," she said again. "Promise you'll never settle for less than what we're throwing away."

***

The pain in her heart didn't fully hit until Solange arrived home in Paris. It came to her during the day, when everything was a reminder of Virgil, and at night, in a dream that continuously left her drained and numb and aching and feverish during the day.

In her dream, she holds hands with Virgil on the steps of the Capitol building. His hand feels warm and real, but his face is flat, like a painting.

"I like your knees," says the painting without moving his lips. "Are you Irish?" He traces the scars on her knees with a black ink pen.

"American, born in Paris," she answers. "I fell off a swing when I was a little girl. Nobody took my open knees seriously, so these scars formed."

"I like scars," he says. "Inside and outside. They're honest."

Then Virgil's gone and she's on a snow-covered mountain desperately searching for something. An eagle flies by and asks what she's looking for.

"Beauty," Solange answers in her dream, and she wants to tell the bird about Byzantine art. The bird laughs, and the mountain shakes with laughter.

***

"You haven't told me what happened between you and Virgil," Solange's mother said, setting the breakfast table a week after her return. "Nobody drops a paid internship at an art school for no reason."

"I don't know what happened." Solange escaped and petted her old dog waiting for his morning walk. She kissed his wrinkled brow. "You snore, old Boy, even when you're awake."

"Boxers do that." Her father snapped the leash on the dog. "Sleep well?"

"I think I'll lie down again."

"Do that, angel." He gave her a quick hug. "It takes me weeks to get over jet lag."

Solange lay on her bed and tried to remember the details of the real day she met Virgil for the first time. I'm confusing everything, she realized. I can't tell memories from dreams.

"I'm not sleeping," she answered the soft knock on her door.

"Have you heard from the young man?" Two steaming mugs in her hands, her mother sat down on the edge of the bed and offered one to Solange.

"He has a new girlfriend." Solange tried to sound neutral. "A friend saw them together and told me. This whole thing . . . it's like a great dream that turned into a nightmare. I know it was, and yet it already isn't real. Only pain is. Every morning when I wake up, I can feel the bad parts. I feel beaten up. Exhausted. And what I can't figure out is, what happened to make it go from good to bad?"

"If he has a new life, accept it, Solange." Her mother stroked Solange's face. "You've spent the past week in bed, moping. It's time you got out!"

The old dog came in, climbed up on the bed, and tried to crawl under the duvet.

"You could walk Boy!" said her mother. "Take him for a run in the Champs de Mars."

"I'll call Daniel."

"The dandy I met last year? Isn't he in Washington?"

"London," said Solange. "He sent me a postcard. And he's not a dandy, Mom. Daniel believes all aspects of life should be art, including the way he dresses, speaks, what he eats . . . it's fun."

She showed her Daniel's card on the night table. On the front, Hampstead Heath; on the back: "Fog is the fifth element. Creating media humdrum for too much dosh. D."

"We're just friends," she added, true to her last meeting with Daniel.

"You've gained weight," her critical mother observed and dragged the slobbering dog off the bed. "You may want to diet and exercise before you meet this epicurean friend."

***

"Am I disturbing something?" Solange asked after Daniel's lazy hello.

"Nothing terribly important," he admitted. "I'm indulging in narcissistic pleasures. My own body in my full-length mirror in Flat 16, Heath Close, Heath Road, Hampstead, London. It's a work of art. My once-teenage-angst-ridden mass, I mean. Fierce discipline and determination transformed that bloated mess into a living classical sculpture. I never showed you pictures of what I used to look like, did I? Try long hair, unshaven, overweight. I keep my current body gorgeous with morning jogs through the Heath. Not the loose-limbed, rolling kind of jog! I concentrate on tight buttocks. Please note: five miles three times a week. I also swim two miles at Hampstead pool twice a week. My weekends are soul days, in case you wonder about the two days unaccounted for. I sing harmonious duets with Jacques Brel, Charles Aznavour, and Robbie Williams when I'm in a poetic mood; Bob Marley, Carlos Santana, Mick Jagger when my batteries need recharging; Bruce Springsteen's almost a childhood friend. He's the voice that keeps me rooted, a contemporary who says all the things about growing up I shouldn't forget."

"You're engaged to be married," Solange mentioned, wondering where his fiancée fit in to that ambitious schedule.

"That's over," said Daniel. "We got too close to the real thing too fast. I need fiction as much as you do."

"I need to see you," said Solange.

"What happened?"

"I left DC."

"He didn't try to stop you," said Daniel. "You need a couple of days in

Venice. I've got work to do in Ravenna over the next months, and I'm treating myself to a weekend in Venice. Join me. Café Florian, Saturday, four o'clock."

"I'll be there."

***

They were seated at the Florian like models for a painting. The orchestra delivered the soundtrack to the often-documented atmosphere, paparazzi searched for faces, and sparkling white implants flashed between wrinkled lips and cake. Daniel poured Limoncello and raised his glass. "To Venice!"

Solange tore her gaze from the dust-covered pigeons that carpeted Piazza San Marco. "I shouldn't have come," she said and peered through Daniel's affectations at herself. "I'm not even really here; I'm stuck in D.C."

"Forget the asshole." Daniel's patience had cracked, and he tried to catch the vulgarism with a shrug.

"I'm trying to."

Daniel opened his arms, embracing the Florian, tired musicians, Italian sunshine, historic buildings, severe sculptures, perfumed ladies, and smartly dressed men.

"Venice is the most beautiful city in the world," he declared. "Love it!" His gaze followed an elegant woman who moved with a graceful limp through the fluttering pigeons to the water.

"Let's look at masks." He pulled Solange up from the chair that seemed to break her and dragged her into the narrow streets behind the piazza. He looked into store windows, searching for the right mask.

"Death glorified," cried Daniel and laughed delightedly at the display of leather and velvet masks in a shop window.

Solange remained outside in the cool alley. Through the narrow glass window, she observed Daniel negotiating with the store owner, but his final purchase was shielded from her view. He emerged with a black velvet box, which he refused to open. "Later. Follow me."

Daniel led her to the Bridge of Sighs. "A palace on one side, a prison on the other," he said. "You're on that bridge, Solange. Which way will you go? Do you want to languish in the prison of memories? Or do you want to live in the palazzo of life with all the different rooms and possibilities?"

He led her through the Doge's Palace, where every room was ornately painted. "If I had the means," he confided, "I would live here with all this beauty, and I would make myself look across at the prison every day to remind myself how lucky I am."

Daniel had taken a room for the night at the Bauer-Grünwald Hotel. Exhausted from hours of walking through Venice, Solange kicked off her heels and buried her sore feet in the thick carpeting while Daniel unzipped her velvet dress. She lay down on the large, satin-covered bed, closed her eyes, and fell instantly into a dream.

She was back in Virgil's room. He wasn't there, but his bed was rumpled. She smoothed the sheets and heard laughter. Solange whipped back the sheets and found a giggling woman hiding under the covers.

Solange woke from her nightmare with a start. A naked man stood by the open balcony doors facing the lagoon, his face hidden by a flat leather mask. The masked man joined Solange on the bed and stroked her bare skin.

"Virgil," Solange cried out as the mask exploded on the high ceiling. "Why did you let me go?"

Daniel ripped off the mask and pulled Solange close to him. "I'm holding you," he said over and over until she cried herself to sleep in his arms.

Again, Solange dreamed of Virgil standing in the snow by the 7-Eleven.

"I'm looking for beauty," she said to him in her dream.

Virgil laughed and crossed the street. She watched him and stood horrified and helpless as his big coat bit into him. Her teeth chattered. She tried to run to Virgil's aid but couldn't move. She stood frozen on the sidewalk as the coat devoured his long fingers, slender neck, and perfect head. Then the coat spread its sleeves and flew off.

***

"A big wool coat ate Virgil," Solange told Daniel on the boat over to Murano the following morning.

"Dali painted stuff like that," said Daniel. "Modern art's punishing you for your passion."

"Virgil punished me for that."

"You were too much for him," said Daniel when they settled in a café. He suggested espresso and pistachio ice cream. "Enjoy earthly pleasures as they come."

"I'm a slave to the past," said Solange. "I love old masters and castle

63

ruins. But even more than the works, I love the memory of having seen them. Maybe this is what is happening now with Virgil? The farther away I am from him, from the actual 'us' of that relationship, the more precious he becomes."

They left the fragile art of Murano glass and returned to Venice. Daniel took Solange to the station and put her on the overnight train back to Paris. He stowed her bag in the rack above her reserved seat and gave her the mask.

"When will I see you again?" Solange stroked the flat face that reminded her of Virgil.

"When you're ready." Daniel repeated his promise: "I'll leave a trail of breadcrumbs."

***

Solange returned to Paris and placed the mask on the wall above her bed. She woke up the following morning and knew Daniel had held her all night long. She took Boy for his morning walk. "I'm getting better," she whispered into the old dog's ticklish ear. "I didn't dream of Virgil."

Solange ordered coffee and a croissant at the foot of the Eiffel Tower and imagined sharing the morning with Daniel. Then she shook her head and sighed. She sipped the hot drink, listened to Boy growl at pigeons he no longer chased, and decided to make a new life for herself in Paris.

***

Two months later, a postcard arrived. On the front, a picture of San Vitale in Ravenna. On the back, a few crumbs: "Captive in a fifteenth-century castle: one man's soul. Ransom: all the grapes in the world. D."

Perfectly Pretty and other love stories

Eugene & Kuki

Johanna Miklós

Eugene

Eugene's fate was in lockstep with his mother's for the first few years of his life. Mona Ehrlich—and Eugene—divorced Frank Ehrlich after 2,192 ironed shirts, 312 Sunday roasts, and 5 consecutive nights waiting in vain for his return from the office. She kept accurate records. Mona Ehrlich wanted a confession of her husband's sins. She had a list of those. She expected hard penance followed by tearful, dramatic, until-death-do-us-part redemption. She had been raised a

Christian and therefore believed in second chances, despite the evidence in numbers. Frank Ehrlich, however, preferred his freedom.

Mona demanded custody of their son, Eugene. Frank complied. She sued for support. Frank fought back. After one year of embarrassingly detailed, intimate, and soul-destroying court appearances, the separation *Ehrlich v. Ehrlich* was stamped by the family court of Hamburg in 1965.

Mother and son moved out of the marital home to a studio apartment in the dull part of Norderstedt. Mona, no longer a stay-at-home wife, rejoined the work force as an accountant. Eugene, now with a working mom, learned to say "Here" during roll call and "Sorry" when he did not want to share a toy at day care. He also got a new, yellow rain jacket and a shiny, red bicycle from Frank.

Then Paul Mahler came and rescued Mona. He took her to his one-bedroom, high-rise luxury apartment in the center of Hamburg. He showed off his view of the port and guided her by the elbow over tomato-red, wall-to-wall carpeting to a chrome-and-steel kitchen. Paul courted Mona over candlelit foie gras dinners served on Meissen china. Brahms concertos—played on Paul's state-of-the-art hi-fi set—accelerated the new romance with their passionate orchestration of simple themes. They eventually kissed on his deep, leather sofa and exchanged vows of love in his steamed-up black marble shower.

Eugene and Mona married Paul Mahler. It was a simple but elegant ceremony. Eugene got his first suit for the occasion and a toy box for the move.

In the first week in his new home, Eugene shared hot cocoa with his teddy bear and accidentally spilled it on the tomato-red carpet. Mona scrubbed, but the stain remained. Then Eugene raced on his shiny bicycle through the flaming desert of his imagination and scratched up the leather sofa that doubled as his bed—for good.

Paul cringed as greasy fingerprints smudged the once crystal-clear view. He stammered apologies to neighbors when a flood caused by the maritime battle between Captain Eugene and the Black Port Monster leaked through the floors. Finally, Paul tripped over a Lego fort and twisted his ankle. The searing pain punctured the cyst of his accumulated frustration at the clothes stuffed into his once tidy drawers and closets; the turbulent invasion of toys on his shelves; the chocolate cookie fed to his cassette player; his refrigerator filled with cartons of milk, cold cuts, and calcium-fortified cheese spreads instead of choice delicacies and champagne; globs of pink toothpaste in his black marble sink; and the silent, embarrassed fumbling that now constituted his sex life.

The brand-new family man exploded. Paul swept Eugene's toys from the shelves, trampled the squealing teddy bear, crushed grinning knights underfoot, shredded pop-up books, and snapped crayons in half. He howled barely comprehensible words as he stumbled from the living room into the bedroom. There, he hurled little rolled-up socks and pale blue underwear across the room. He ripped Superman and Babar T-shirts, hand-knit sweaters, and Eugene's wedding suit from their Mickey Mouse hangers and threw them, along with embroidered jeans, striped shorts, boots, sandals, and Eugene's glossy yellow slicker, onto the floor. Spent, Paul collapsed on his bed and Mona shut the door.

Eugene huddled beside the scratched leather sofa and quietly placed his broken toys in their box. Despite the closed door, he clearly heard Paul's sobs and his mother's soothing voice.

"I can't live like this," Eugene heard him say. "I need romance, my love. I need us to be us."

Mona finally came from the bedroom and pulled Eugene from the floor onto her lap. She rocked her son and caressed his head. "It will all be fine," she said. "You know I love you."

Meanwhile, Paul Mahler made decisions on the phone. He signed little Eugene up for boarding school, effective the same day. He also enlisted the help of relatives with a house by the North Sea for healthy, child-appropriate vacations.

"It's an excellent school," Mona told her son. "I'll come visit on Wednesday afternoons. We'll have lots of fun together."

***

Two years later, Eugene's healthy summer vacation with step-in-laws ended abruptly after only three weeks. The retired couple, who treated Eugene well, called him in from his dugout on the windy beach and told him to pack his suitcase.

"What did I do?" Eugene was certain he had behaved well.

"Nothing," they each said and told him his mother would explain everything.

They drove him to the train, paid for his ticket, and installed him in an empty car. They gave him cash in an envelope for a taxi home from the station in Hamburg.

"Paul is going to be really mad at me," said Eugene and held on to the couple's hands. "Please, let me stay. I won't do it again. I promise."

The man was about to speak, but the woman put a hand over his mouth. "It's not our place."

So, a few hours later, Eugene stood in front of the apartment he had been expelled from two years earlier and rang the bell. A man in a dark gray suit with a black tie opened the door and let him in. The apartment looked as he remembered it, but for the sound of wailing. Eugene followed the high-pitched sound to the bedroom. There, Eugene observed two soft-spoken men—also in dark gray suits—respectfully tear Paul Mahler from his mother's arms.

They lowered Paul into a velvet-lined coffin and snapped the lid shut—regrettably, on Eugene's fingers.

***

A small number of mourners followed Eugene and Mona from the chapel to an open grave. They stood in a semicircle behind the weeping widow and the boy in the too-tight wedding-turned-funeral suit, his hands wrapped in thick bandages. Former colleagues, immediate neighbors—including those of the flooding incident—and Mahler cousins stood in the hot July sun and listened to a recording of Brahm's "Funeral Hymn," followed by a brief prayer. Then, each in turn and without haste, they shoveled earth on the lowered coffin. Each spoke words of condolence as they shook Mona's hand. The men squeezed Eugene's shoulders, and the women kissed his cheek. Then the mourners left the cemetery. Mother and son stood alone and waited at the grave until Eugene's father arrived.

Frank Ehrlich, whom Eugene had last seen during the Christmas holidays, treated him to a milkshake with a straw and slip-on shoes.

"Am I going back to boarding school?" said Eugene.

Frank Ehrlich shook his head. He told Eugene to be nice to his mother and returned him a few hours later with a fifty-Mark bill stuffed into the breast pocket of his too-small suit.

***

Six weeks later, the bandages came off Eugene's hands. His little fingers looked shrunken—white and stiff. The doctors prescribed physical therapy.

Eugene and Mona then gave up Paul's high-rise apartment. They loaded the good furniture into a van and moved back to the depressed part of Norderstedt. There, Mona complained bitterly about the musty kitchen with a view of the garbage chute, and at night she buried her face in the leather sofa that now served as her bed and wept.

There, Eugene learned that his fingers would remain short and crooked. Again, Mona buried her face in the sofa and wept.

Mona rejoined the work force as an accountant. Eugene hid his claw-like hands that seemed to shrink as his body grew.

Eugene survived his mother's mourning and the bleakness of Norderstedt because he was determined to be a dragon slayer, then a pianist, and later a volleyball player or a surgeon. Despite his hands. He finally decided to become all those things and more. Eugene cast off the widow's lot on the first day of his nineteenth year. He slammed the door on Mona's grief, his deformed fingers hidden deep in his trouser pockets, and set out to make his dreams come true.

***

Eugene had an offer from a small garrison town straight out of drama school. The citizens—intellectuals who emphasized inner values to the detriment of such superficial virtues as cleanliness—invested in the arts. They hired Eugene to mime the singer, dancer, victor, victim, lover, son, and agreed to honor his performance with beer, Schnapps, and swooning applause. They also provided lodgings with a respected landlady who led multiple lives and eavesdropped at every door.

A few weeks after Eugene moved into a room on the second floor of the two-family semi-detached, he saw a hearse stop in front of the house. He crept down the stairs and stood in the open door to the landlady's filthy basement apartment. His child-sized fingers safe in the lowest corners of his trouser pockets, he watched as men in dark gray suits lowered the late husband into a coffin and carried him under a false name out of the house.

"It's not his fault," the landlady told Eugene. "His parents changed Adolf to Adelt right after the war."

That same evening, Eugene discovered his father, whom he hadn't seen since Paul Mahler's funeral, in the glass-and-chrome theater lobby. Frank Ehrlich treated him to dinner, beer, and Schnapps and gave him cash for decent shoes. He mentioned a new wife and showed Eugene pictures of her children.

"They're so small," said Eugene. "Don't send them away."

***

Eugene met Kuki two days later. He'd been rehearsing a romantic comedy with the slim blonde actress for a week but had been unaware of her until her wide-set blue eyes flashed panic as she forgot her lines. Eugene approached, gently stroked her flushed cheek with his tiny fingers, and lowered his lips.

***

Katlinka

"I don't want to go!" shouted Katlinka, crouched behind the bathroom door. She gnawed her palms and clung to the helpless eyes of her grandmother. "Help me, Baba."

Katlinka saw her father over her grandmother's shoulder. Brown liquid dribbled from the corners of his pinched mouth. She was too young to know that the last cup of coffee in Prague tasted as bitter to Pavel as the years of hushed and hurried sex in the narrow bed behind a curtain in his mother-in-law's living room; that his good suit reeked of the old woman because it had to share the only peg behind the entrance door with her musty, gray coat; that his small musician's salary paid for meals but never amounted to enough for the necessary bribe to advance

85

on the list of home-seekers. Pavel lived where he did not want to live, played notes he did not want to play, and hid his real music deep in his soul.

"I'm going," Pavel turned to his wife. "Right now! I won't let that brat ruin my life!" He had dreamed of this escape since he was a teenager. He had planned it in earnest since the day after he married, when he added to his yearning for music in the free West the urgent need to be far away from the mocking look of his mother-in-law over the breakfast table. It had taken years of secret letters to make arrangements, and now, with a child, he had far too much baggage.

"Baba, make Katlinka go! Pavel's leaving without us," the mother pleaded with the child's grandmother.

Then Baba pushed her only grandchild from her soft arms and

Katlinka's head hit the rim of the rusty old tub.

***

Katlinka woke to music beating through a fat bandage around her head.

"We're in Vienna!" Her mother kissed her cheek.

She followed her mother along a brightly-lit corridor with large photographs of smiling men and women playing the piano, cello, and violin. Katlinka stepped over open instrument cases, edged past a long table covered with sheet music and discarded hats and coats, and came to a room filled with people snapping their fingers. She peered between swaying bodies and saw her father sweating into his trumpet. For the first time in her life, Katlinka saw her father happy.

But the wave of euphoric, wild, glowing parties to welcome the new dissident came to a quiet end. Pavel couldn't find steady work. The occasional guest gig barely paid for their living expenses. Katlinka's mother applied for a work permit.

"I need to work!" she said. "I have my little girl to feed."

"You have a husband," the civil servant pointed out. "Your husband has a permit."

"He's a musician." Katlinka's mother apologized for bringing her child and for the mud stains on his floor. Embarrassed by her rumbling stomach, she also confessed to poverty. "We had such dreams!" she said. "Now I see bills and I have no money. Please, I beg of you!"

The servant of the free West stamped her application: "ABGELEHNT—

DENIED." Katlinka's mother hugged her daughter and cried.

Soon she packed Katlinka's clothes and toys—gifts from generous and well-meaning people who had welcomed Pavel and his family with open arms. However, the "prodigy" they had such high hopes for turned out to be a "choleric," "difficult to manage," and "greedy foreigner" who actually expected to be paid!

Katlinka and her mother took the tram and then a bus out of Vienna and were met by "Uncle Manfred" and "Aunt Julia." The mother made two promises before she got back on the bus without her daughter: "As soon as your father has work, we will be together as a family again," and, "I will visit you as often as I can."

Her mother kept the second promise. Every second Sunday, Katlinka would wait behind the glass-paneled door of Uncle Manfred's house. But Aunt Julia, much taller than Katlinka, always saw the mother first and said, "Guck mal, wer da kommt!"—"Look who's coming!"—as she opened the door. Katlinka, who spoke little German, heard "Kuckmal," which she mistook to be her new name. In her young mouth, it became "Kuki," and later, when she understood the mistake, she decided to keep Kuki anyway.

"I'm always looking and not seeing," she explained to Aunt Julia. "It's a good name for me."

Kuki rejected music lessons, although she had perfect pitch, because her mother couldn't keep the first promise. She read about Pavel's fame in Aunt Julia's magazines, but by then he was no longer her mother's husband, and, by association, he was also no longer her father.

Kuki chose dance despite big feet and tall bones. She never cut her straight blonde hair, despite girls with short curls assuring her that if only she cut it, her mother would take her home. Kuki didn't believe them because her mother kept her second promise for many years. She came every second Sunday until Kuki was "almost all grown-up," "definitely old enough," and could understand about a new husband and soon a new child. Aunt Julia and Uncle Manfred legally adopted Kuki when she was thirteen.

***

Eugene and Kuki

"A touching moment!" shouted the artistic director from his seat in the third row center. "But I'd also like to hear some text!"

"The text sucks!" Eugene hid his fists in the pockets of his old linen jacket.

"Ehrlich! My office. Now!" bellowed the artistic director. He swallowed the last bite of the third hard-boiled egg of his second breakfast as he stormed to his office. Eugene and Kuki left the stage and made their way through the wings, dressing rooms, and greenroom to the administrative offices. Eugene knocked and stepped into the office. Kuki stayed in the corridor. She leaned against the poster-covered wall and waited her turn.

***

"Leave the child here."

"I'm not going without Katlinka! She's coming with us!" Her mother had packed Katlinka's few belongings into a plastic bag. "I want my daughter to grow up in the West! Free!"

"Free?" Baba wept. "How can she be free among those murderers?"

Katlinka's grandmother and her mother had faced each other in the cramped confines of the one-bedroom apartment that had been home to Katlinka and a prison for Pavel. Anger versus fear—at least that's what Kuki later supposed. That, and her beloved grandmother's memory of the great war that made her a widow versus a young woman's hope for the future.

***

The door to the artistic director's office slammed, and Eugene stood before Kuki.

"Had breakfast yet?" asked Eugene. "He doesn't want to see you. All my fault.

It's apparently not my place to criticize authors. Anyway, rehearsals are canceled for today."

They went to a small café near the theater, with greasy tables and lace-curtained windows. Once seated, she ordered coffee and rolls, and he added a beer and Schnapps. Then they talked about struggling mothers and absent fathers. Eugene looked out and saw a mud-spattered hearse roll by. He clenched his short fingers.

"You know what a stroke looks like?" He promptly demonstrated what he had seen.

"Where do you get that?"

"My stepfather. He dropped dead when I was seven. I wanted to know what he felt like dead, and they slammed the coffin lid on my fingers. That's why I have crippled fingers."

"Did he hurt you?" Kuki asked as she paid their bill.

"He broke all my toys and sent me away." Eugene plucked at his eyebrows and tried to remember the text she had forgotten. All he could think of was the smell of hard-boiled eggs.

"In the end, we're all the same." He helped Kuki into her coat.

"Abandoned," she said about their childhoods.

"I mean dead." Eugene pushed the café door open. Immediately, the cold wind stabbed him through his thin linen jacket. He gasped.

The wind also lifted Kuki's long hair, and she laughed as she caught it with both hands and wound it around her neck like a scarf.

"Is Kuki beautiful?" Eugene asked the air and the street as he squinted into the white winter sun. "I bet you have always been beautiful."

They walked through quiet streets to the row of attached houses and stopped before the one draped in mourning.

"I don't need anybody," said Eugene before he opened the door.

Kuki followed Eugene past mumbling mourners and the tearful landlady and up creaking stairs to the second floor, as she had years ago followed her grandmother to their room. She had shared Baba's huge, wood-frame bed covered with colorful pillows that smelled of cinnamon, duck feathers, wax candles, and rosewater. Every morning, Baba had first kissed Katlinka and then the photograph of a young soldier, and every night Baba had locked the door on Pavel's rage and her mother's cries and tears.

Eugene's room, bare but for the legal minimum of one bed, one table, and one chair, smelled of too many lodgers.

"Like a hotel room," observed Kuki. "You have nothing personal in here."

"Now I do. I have you." He hid his stunted fingers in his pockets and stared past Kuki through the dirty window at the brilliant white sun. "It's better if you find someone else," he said to her silence and added, "I can't love anyone."

Then he looked at her and saw her wide mouth, round chin, and delicate nose decorated with tiny freckles. It should look heavy on such a slender neck, he thought. She's very pretty, Eugene decided. He lowered his eyes and stared at the tips of her high-heeled, elegant shoes. Big feet, he thought.

"I need to sleep," said Kuki.

He turned his back and listened as she locked the door, undressed, and crawled under the covers.

"You need me," she said.

Eugene's twisted fingers ached to be held, but he chose to keep them hidden, deep in pockets, behind his back, below tabletops, between his knees, even under his thighs. Kuki fell asleep. She slept as she had as a child, safe from tears and rage behind the locked door.

***

After two more confrontations with the artistic director and a bitter battle with the landlady who wanted morality where Eugene demanded privacy, Kuki and Eugene left the garrison town. They toured main stages offering youth and strong, well-trained voices to houses with a solid reputation for excellence, places where Art—capital *A*—was played and sung, where audiences sought statements and everybody was looking for a profit. For almost three years, Kuki and Eugene traveled from town to town.

And though handsome, young, male actors are scarce, still Eugene's parts grew smaller, the quantities of beer and Schnapps bigger. He buried his hands more and more deeply in the frayed pockets of his jacket. "Let me accomplish my fate," Eugene railed at Kuki when he was not drunk enough to be beyond macho pride. "Let me die alone."

Since young actresses abound, Kuki stopped being an actress. Struggling to make ends meet, she taught in fitness studios where she danced in front of large mirrors and was rewarded with applause and a few crisp bills per lesson by stretching- and jazz-dance-enthusiast mothers and secretaries.

"Your work keeps me alive," said Eugene.

"I keep the wolves at bay," Kuki answered.

She was the breadwinner who provided morning coffee and the bed they shared at night. He didn't notice her remove his shoes and belt, jacket and socks. He didn't feel her hold his crooked hands. He was oblivious to her tears on his deformed fingers pressed against her cheek as she recreated the first time he had touched her.

***

"Your history is the history of your own underestimation," Kuki said to Eugene.

"What kind of shit are you reading now?" He didn't really want to know. A theater festival director had auditioned Eugene and immediately saw in him the young hero for the romantic Schiller drama, the handsome prince in the children's fairy tale, and the romantic baritone for the musical. To the town committee sponsoring the festival, the director described Eugene Ehrlich as "A boy with a great future, a highly-talented asset to this ensemble, and a bargain, because he is not yet famous."

"Rehearsals start tomorrow at ten." He leafed through the script. He was learning the part of the young hero who falls in love with a commoner and has to fight the intrigues of his aristocratic father.

Kuki thought of the first time she had stood on a stage and played the part of Eugene's lover. She remembered the look in his eyes when she had forgotten her lines; she remembered how he had gently touched her cheek. This would also be their first separation, as there had been no work for her in this little town.

Eugene counted her freckles. "Thirty-five, that's three more than last week."

"They go away in the winter," insisted Kuki.

"They're always there," he said. "I wouldn't know you without them."

"I'll go shopping," declared Kuki and put away the women's magazine she had been reading. "I might buy myself a new dress." She didn't need to tell him that she hadn't bought a new dress since they had left the garrison town.

"We're becoming a bourgeois couple," said Eugene. "The man works and the woman shops. It's a first for us."

"I could just unpack."

"I'll check out the town." Eugene pocketed the script and disappeared.

Kuki unpacked their cases, made a grocery list, and rearranged the furniture. Then she wrote a letter to Aunt Julia with greetings to Uncle Manfred.

At midnight she set out to look for Eugene.

***

"I'm croaking here!" cried Eugene as he returned from the seventeenth rehearsal, as he had from the sixteenth, fifteenth, and fourteenth. He slammed his fraying script down on the table.

"All . . ." prompted Kuki.

"All the same!" shouted Eugene. "A-
ll s-peak po-lish-ed words! Vapid eyes!
Uncontrolled gestures! No sap! No sap!"
He ran out the door again into the warm
summer afternoon. Kuki slipped on her
sandals and followed him to his favorite
pub.

"Hello, Kuki!" Peter, the young
owner of the pub, had lived in Munich and
was a fan of all things artistic. He had
returned from his big-city adventure to his
native town, settled down with a bride-to-
be and regulars like Eugene. He served
Kuki a glass of sparkling water at the
sidewalk table where she always sat and
offered her a cigarette. "Eugene says
you've found work."

Behind the bar, his hard-working
fiancée kept an eye on beers, slowly filling
large glasses. In front of the counter,
Eugene rocked back and forth on a tall

stool. He had empty shot glasses lined up in front of him and his eyes fixed on the television suspended from the ceiling .

"A dance camp for children," Kuki told Peter. "It's in an old castle outside of Munich. It should be fun." She observed Eugene through the open pub door, afraid to leave him alone for two weeks with Peter's beer and Schnapps and those who would want to mother him and take him away from her.

"I'll keep an eye on him," said Peter. He went back inside to watch the soccer game and have a beer with Eugene. Kuki opened a magazine to the horoscope page. She always read Eugene's first. According to this astrologer, he was born under a sign haunted by demons and needed a supportive partner, preferably Cancer or Pisces. Kuki had Cancer as her rising sign.

Eugene finished his second beer. No goal had been marked yet.

Anna, one of Peter's regulars, arrived in a new, red polyester pantsuit that stretched over her dimpled thighs. Anna ordered her first Campari as Benny, another regular, came from his day shift and joined Kuki at the outdoor table. "What can I tempt you with?"

"Lay off my woman!" shouted Eugene without taking his eyes off the playing field on the small screen.

"Didn't mean anything bad," muttered Benny and heaved himself in a slow and tired movement from the sidewalk chair onto the high barstool next to Anna.

"Who's playing?" Anna squinted at the screen. "Wolfgang's racing that hot little car of his," she added. "If he won, he'll throw a couple of rounds."

"He throws rounds when he loses, too," remarked Benny. Eugene grabbed his fourth beer and joined Kuki during the halftime break in the match.

"I'll call you here in the evenings. After the show.. Peter said he'll start serving sandwiches during the festival."

"My father was here," said Eugene. "He asked if I was hungry and gave me this for shoes." He pulled three one-hundred-Mark bills from his crumpled jacket pockets.

"You could use a new pair."

"It's bad luck to switch shoes during a show." Eugene wore the same trousers and jacket as the day they met. "Quality lasts," he told people who suggested a change.

"You keep the money," he told Kuki. "We probably owe rent or tab or something." He finished his beer and returned to the second half of the game.

Kuki folded the bills and put them in her wallet. She would give them to Peter to pay for Eugene's food and drink while she was away. She returned to her magazine and tuned out the bar and the soccer match.

The final whistle was blown, and the bride-to-be turned off the set. Wolfgang arrived with a gold-sprayed laurel wreath around his neck, followed by friends and colleagues. Peter hung the wreath over the television set, opened a new bottle of Schnapps, and started new drafts. Slow drafts, Eugene insisted. Seven minutes slow, Peter assured them all. Wolfgang kissed Anna and told her that she looked gorgeous.

"Your old lady should see this!" Benny pointed up at the wreath.

"You're married?" Eugene wondered, either at Benny's grammar or at the relationship between Wolfgang and Anna.

"We're the club of the happily divorced," said Anna and raised her glass to include Wolfgang and Benny. "Cheers!"

"Divorce sucks!" snarled Eugene but raised his glass all the same.

Outside, the sun set and Kuki felt a chill. She considered going inside but wasn't in the mood for bawdy jokes and liquor.

"May I?" a young woman with large rhinestone earrings stood by the table. "My name is Lisa. I'm getting myself a glass of wine. Can I get you anything?"

"Okay, dry white," Kuki said. She knew the young woman was Eugene's lover in the play.

The raucous group at the bar greeted Lisa and invited her to join them for the next round. Lisa declined and ordered two glasses of white wine from the bride-to-be.

"I thought you'd be in bed by this time," said Eugene.

"You think about me?" Lisa raised her eyebrows at him mockingly. "Your eyes are bloodshot." She picked up the two glasses and went back outside.

"All the same!" Eugene called after her.

"Who's the same?" Anna asked Eugene, who ignored her and stared instead at Lisa and Kuki settled at a sidewalk table.

"Thank you." Kuki went to hand Lisa money.

"My treat." Lisa refused Kuki's offer. "I wanted to talk to you. Your name is Kuki, right? Right. I'm playing opposite Eugene, but you know that! He doesn't make things easy for me. Not at all! It's a difficult part and he's . . . well, he's not there . . ."

"He's a very gifted actor—"

"He just declaims his text!" Lisa threw up her arms in a silent commanding pose and dropped them again. "We're not doing *Julius Caesar*! Admittedly, he has a good voice and formulates well. But that's radio! He struts around me, waves his arms, grabs his eyebrows, exits, and nothing has happened. I look at him and there's . . . nobody, if you see what I mean. I can't work like that. I want to do honest work, and this is a difficult part."

It had grown dark, and Kuki could not determine the color of Lisa's eyes. Something like brown, she decided. Brown slits, cat eyes with small lines that would become deep wrinkles.

Eugene examined his coaster and counted the strokes that tallied his tab. Nine. He was finishing his ninth beer.

"My treat." Wolfgang grabbed all the coasters on the counter. "Tonight, all divorce victims are my guests."

"Best never to get married," came from Benny. "Why get stuck with one?"

"Old pig!" scolded the bride-to-be.

"You're an exception," said Benny and then couldn't think of why she would be.

"Yes!" Eugene rose to Benny's rescue. "You're a fine catch for my friend Peter."

"Flirt!"

"Am I attractive?" Anna stopped Eugene from leaving the pub.

"I should go home," Eugene answered. "I hate red. Red carpets, red bicycles, and especially middle-aged women in red suits."

"You're afraid of life," said Anna, and to Benny she added, "Alcohol gives me great insight into others. I wish it gave me the next lottery numbers, too."

"We're all wearing masks!" announced Eugene.

"Like at Mardi Gras?" asked Anna.

"Like in your office," Eugene hissed into her flushed face. "Where you play secretary and salute your bosses' orders. Like on stage where I sell my ass. Like in the pub where you offer your painted mouth to any man! Just masks! All the same!"

"He's drunk," said Benny.

"Can't stand life sober," Eugene admitted and dove into the lavatory.

The bride-to-be nudged Peter. "Will he be coming out of there again?"

"Give him time," Peter said to his bride-to-be.

Outside, Kuki said the same thing to Lisa.

"Does he even know other people exist?" Lisa asked without expecting a response. "It's his entrance and his exit and how a line is fed to him. We're all having a really hard time with Eugene, and he's in almost every scene. The scenes without him are doing fine, in case you're wondering if the whole cast is dysfunctional. You know he'll be playing opposite me in the next production too. It's going to be really no fun at all unless something changes. I have a great working relationship with everybody in the cast—"

"Masks." Eugene dropped into the seat between Kuki and Lisa. "You're all masks. I see the masks. Pretty, painted masks to hide heartless faces."

"And what are you? You're also an actor. This is about being professional. It's not about your private life," said Lisa.

"I'm unwanted and invisible. The only one who sees me and still won't leave me is Kuki."

Kuki tried to laugh with him, but the laughter wouldn't sound. She started crying. Lisa gave her a tissue and hissed at Eugene, "You're a mean alcoholic on top of everything else."

"Never when I'm working." He looked for his trouser pockets that seemed to have disappeared, gave up, and hid his hands in his lap. "Five Schnapps and my body's numb. Nine beers and eight Schnapps and nothing really matters. Why am I explaining this to you? I'll tell Wolfgang. Of all the masks in there, he's the one who'd understand."

Kuki wiped her nose and picked up her wallet, magazine, and house keys. "I'm going home."

"I'll follow in a moment. I think Lisa here has a bone to pick with me." Eugene turned up his face for Kuki's kiss and then watched her walk away, her long blonde hair like a burning torch visible under the street lamps until she turned left into an alley.

Lisa put her hands flat on the table. "I want a really tender moment with the pretend lover I will fight for and then lose for forty-five performances."

Inside the pub, Peter turned on the jukebox and invited his bride-to-be to dance. Benny focused on his beer. Wolfgang went to a woman in a black, strapless summer dress and twirled her into his arms. Anna decided to leave.

"What do you want me to do?" Eugene made an effort not to slur his words.

"Caress." Lisa lifted her hands off the table and held them palms up.

"I have ugly hands." Eugene held his up for inspection. Lisa licked her index finger and slowly traced it along his muscular lower arm and strong wrist, over a fleshy palm, and finally scratched his crooked stumps with her sharp nails. Eugene moaned.

"Are you two lovers?" Anna stopped at the sidewalk table.

"Should go with Anna," Eugene stammered and stood up. "Anna, my red salvation!" He kissed Lisa gently on the forehead and then murmured into her ear, "Could be dangerous with you. Can't hurt Kuki, you know?"

"Well?" Anna pulled Eugene's arm. "Coming, or what?"

"Shut up!" Eugene shook Anna off. "Thish . . . *this* you don't understand." Eugene struggled with his words and his balance and made another attempt. "This is actors working!"

Eugene collapsed on the sidewalk.

"Closing," Peter announced as he followed all the patrons who left the bar to stand around Eugene.

"Someone should call Kuki," suggested Benny.

"I'll drop him off," said Wolfgang and pulled Eugene up over his shoulder. "She's waiting for him."

Perfectly Pretty and other love stories

Johanna Miklós

Magariah's Flaw

Johanna Miklós

I am not fond of travel, yet I find myself regularly wedged into a smelly, scratchy seat with a more or less pleasant traveler (read thin and quiet as opposed to obese, verbose, or the supreme torture: both of the latter) to my left or my right. In any circumstance other than transport, the threat of a stranger one inch from my body for up to eight hours would prompt a handbag dive for pepper spray, a cry for help, or a restraining order. I don't believe in the costly fable of "luxury ten feet ahead" but make sure I have an aisle seat on what my mother calls the "winged pigpen."

On my last flight, I sat next to a perfectly groomed young woman with huge brown eyes. She looked like she belonged on the cover of a fashion magazine. I half expected to find her sporting some incredibly expensive outfit or reclining against a luxury car in the glossy I had picked up at the airport. She sat quietly reading the in-flight magazine. When we reached cruising altitude, she ordered water from the steward and minded her own business while I sipped my five-dollar Bloody Mary and flipped through endless pages of advertising in quest of an article.

"Cute, isn't he?" she suddenly said. Her soft, southern voice perfectly matched her lightly tanned skin and the long, slim finger that pointed at a full-page ad for an aftershave. It was a black-and-white photograph of Adonis wrestling a massive black steer to the ground.

"Drop-dead gorgeous!" I laughed and couldn't stop myself from adding, "I wonder how much airbrushing that took?"

"Oh, Magariah really looks like that," she said.

"You know him?"

She nodded and then held out her hand. "Matu."

I introduced myself and had to ask, "Are you a model too?"

"As a teenager. It's much more competitive for girls than boys. There's always the next new face."

"How old is he?"

"Thirty."

"It must be fun to be this handsome," I thought aloud. "Who is going to say no?"

125

"Everybody," she sighed, and her silver chandelier earrings clicked as she shook her head.

If you haven't seen the ad, here's a description of the man: flawless skin, perfect male musculature on long limbs, a chiseled face seen in profile with a perfectly straight nose, an eyebrow arched like a wing over an eye framed by thick, long lashes, and a mouth that's both full-lipped and firm.

"People must line up just to watch him breathe!" I insisted and flagged down the steward to order another overpriced drink.

"Funny that you talk about breathing," Matu said and proceeded to tell me the beautiful man's life story.

Magariah was born in New York to a couple that already had three pale, blue-blooded, wispy-haired daughters. The mother adored him like all mothers adore baby boys. His sisters tormented him like all sisters torment heirs to the throne. His father planned to take him hunting-fishing-golfing as soon as he was old enough. When he turned three, he was sent to the Montessori school his sisters had attended. By the end of the first day, no child would play with him.

"He was too rough," I guessed from my own experience with Montessori and their emphasis on kindness as a virtue.

Again, the earrings clicked. "Magariah's gentle."

"He stinks," a little girl told Magariah's mother when she came to get him and found him alone in the back of the room.

"Magariah will go home now and take a long bath," the teacher told the class, "and tomorrow we will all play with Magariah."

His mother took him home and announced that he was too young for school. They kept him home until first grade.

"Ladies and gentlemen, this is the captain speaking," the plane's intercom system interrupted Matu's story and bored us with flight details.

"Then what happened?" I was impatient to hear the rest.

When Magariah turned six, he was enrolled in the same school his father and both grandfathers had attended. At the end of the first day, the teacher handed him a note for his mother.

"Make sure you give this note to your mother. Cleanliness is something we all must learn at home."

Magariah went home, handed the note to his mother, and watched her blush and bite her lip. They hired a tutor. Magariah was to be homeschooled.

"Hyperactive sweat glands," interjected the hitherto quiet mouse from the window seat. "Sorry," he added as we both turned to stare at him. "Couldn't help overhearing."

Matu nodded, raised her shoulders in a there-you-have-it gesture, and fell silent. The food cart came by. She turned down their plastic-coated offering; the mouse accepted his and took only the brownie from the packaging; I swilled the salad, sandwich, cheese, and brownie down with a third drink.

"In the main cabin, we will now be showing . . ." The intercom instructed us to lower the blinds for better viewing and gave us a choice of Spanish- or English-

129

language sound if we agreed to pay for headphones. All three of us declined the offer. The trays were whisked away. I leaned forward to see what the intrusive chap in the window seat was up to. He had closed his eyes.

"Then what happened?" I whispered to Matu.

She gave a quick look at the man to her right and then continued in a low voice.

The tutor they found was a young man with a degree in education and a strong belief in physical exercise to promote blood circulation to the brain.

"Before we get to the nitty-gritty of reading, writing, and arithmetic, we're going to make sure that we have a clear head," he announced the very first morning and rolled out two yoga mats. He took off his shoes and told Magariah to

130

follow his example. As soon as Magariah's shoes came off, the tutor gasped, gagged, and ran from the room.

"His feet stank," I realized. "Not the whole kid."

There were many tutors over the years, and all were forbidden to ask Magariah to take off his shoes.

"Our brother stinks so bad, we can't have friends over!" his sisters complained and blamed him for their miserable social lives.

"There's no cure?" I wondered.

"They tried everything," said Matu. Magariah washed his feet every hour. He soaked his feet in salt water and vinegar water; he soaked them in hot water and in cold water. They bought every lotion and powder on the market. Magariah tried every diet, swallowed pills, and drank exotic concoctions. Nothing helped. When

131

he was home, he had to change socks every hour when he washed his feet so that his family could tolerate his presence. Then Magariah hit puberty and the problem grew worse. The stink from his feet became a stench that not even shoes could contain. He couldn't go to stores, restaurants, libraries, or the cinema. Even outside, anyone who stood next to him for a few minutes would notice the nauseating odor and walk away. Very far away.

"That's horrible. Did he have any friends?"

Magariah barely had a family, said Matu. He started running. It was the only exercise he could do that kept him away from people. As long as he was in motion, nobody would notice his problem. He literally ran through puberty straight into the lens of a fashion photographer doing a shoot in Central Park. The photographer showed the photo to Margarete at the Wolff modeling agency. She immediately wanted to meet the boy.

"How old was he by then?"

Eighteen. The photographer found Magariah running his usual laps in Central Park the next morning and stopped him. He handed Magariah a copy of the photograph and a card from the Wolff agency.

Magariah's sisters were amazed. Their smelly brother a model? They secretly showed the picture to their friends, who all thought he was gorgeous.

Magariah put on new socks and new shoes for his interview with Margarete Wolff. He was shown to her elegant office, where she welcomed him with mad hand signals.

"Sday back," she croaked through a wad of tissues. "I haf a cold."

She peered at him, liked what she saw, set up a portfolio shoot with a renowned photographer, and promised him a brilliant career.

"She couldn't smell him because she had a cold," the mouse interrupted. "Colds cause temporary anosmia."

"Are you a doctor?"

"As a matter of fact . . ." He grinned and then held his hand out to Matu. "I'm Fritz. Please don't stop telling your story. I love the way you imitate all these voices."

I also asked Matu to continue, and she agreed after Fritz promised not to interrupt anymore.

Two days later, Margarete summoned her assistant.

"The photographer von't vork vith the new boy," Margarete sniffed, her swollen, red nose quivering with suppressed sneezes. "He says the boy sdinks. Go there. I don't vork vith hysteric photographers."

The assistant grabbed a cab downtown and met the photographer pacing and smoking on the street.

"I'll have to have the place fumigated," he raged. "Is this some kind of sick joke? The kid's up there stinkin' up the place. Margarete's nuts if she thinks that's funny."

The assistant rushed up the stairs and found Magariah in the studio covered in blood. He had one bare foot up on a stool and was hacking away at it with an X-Acto knife.

"Get out. Get out of here!" he screamed at the assistant as he continued to mutilate his foot. The assistant tried to disarm him, but Magariah was too strong and just pushed her away.

"They are ruining my life," he sobbed.

She called an ambulance. It took three men to subdue Magariah.

The next day, the assistant went to the hospital to check on him. She was sent to the psychiatric wing where she found him tied to his bed. Both the nurses who changed the bandage on his foot and the doctor wore hazmat masks.

"What a scene," said Fritz the mouse. "I've heard of stinky cases but never encountered one myself. In the healthcare field, we're used to pretty offensive odors."

"You promised not to interrupt," I hissed at the mouse.

He blushed and coughed. "Sorry."

Matu continued her story.

"Go away," said Magariah to Margarete Wolff's assistant. "You stopped me this time, but you can't be there all the time."

"That kind of talk will get you institutionalized," the doctor said and left the room.

The assistant sat down next to Magariah and explained her belief that the gods had acted fairly.

"Fair? How can this be fair? I don't have a single friend. I've never been on a date. I can't even go to college. I have to stay in my room and take correspondence classes!"

The assistant went to find the doctor. A few minutes later, a full-size mirror was brought into the room. The doctor untied Magariah and, with the assistant's help, pulled him up from the bed and led him hobbling to the mirror.

"Have you ever looked at yourself?" the assistant asked.

Magariah shook his head and then reluctantly looked in the mirror.

"You're perfect. You have perfect proportions, medically and aesthetically. The gods had to do something to keep you humble."

At this, Magariah finally smiled, and the assistant and the doctor caught their breath. "When Magariah smiles, he is absolutely irresistible," Matu finished her story.

"How can he not have known?" I asked.

Matu shrugged. "Who would have told him? They all focused on his odor."

Then she excused herself and left me alone with the mouse.

"May I see the picture?" he asked. I handed him the magazine. "I wouldn't mind looking like that," he finally said. "But I probably wouldn't have gone to med school if I did."

I was surprised to hear him say that and asked him to explain.

"Most of us get an education to compensate for something: lack of beauty, breeding, or money. If you have all three like this chap . . ."

I could see his point. I decided to ask him a medical question. "I'm wondering why the assistant didn't mind the smell."

"Kallmann syndrome," said Fritz, "but ask Matu."

Matu returned to her seat between us, and I did.

"Magariah wondered about the same thing," said Matu.

The assistant then confessed her big secret: she was born without a sense of smell. This was the first time in her life she was happy about it. Without a sense of smell, life can be challenging.

"Did they find a cure?" I asked. "Someone must be working with him."

"Not yet," she said. "The assistant booked a studio and took Magariah's photos herself. She's the only photographer he's worked with ever since."

"Are you friends with this photographer?" I asked.

"I am the photographer," Matu admitted and blushed. "I'm a fashion and ad photographer. I just did a shoot in LA."

"With Magariah?"

"No. He won't travel. We work in a studio in Connecticut."

Matu finished her story just as we approached New York. I lost sight of both Matu and Fritz as I made my way through the terminal but instantly spotted Magariah as I stood at the top of the escalator to the crowded baggage claim area. He stood, his arms crossed over his chest, a good ten-foot radius of empty space around him. His face was blank until a tall woman broke from the crowd. It was Matu. She threw her arms around him. Then I saw his smile; it was the most electric smile I have ever seen.

"A beautiful couple," said Fritz suddenly behind me on the escalator.

"Can you imagine their children?"

"No," said Fritz the doctor, "and we don't have to. Kallmann syndrome also means Matu is sterile."

Johanna Miklós

Ophelia Rekindled

Johanna Miklós

Ophelia, immobile witness to the primal beam splitting sea from sky, stares spellbound through open balcony doors. Outside, black giants shake their arms in the widening cut of blood-red dawn. Ophelia holds her breath. The gnarled tree monsters uproot, reach through the balcony doors, and grab her with their thorny tentacles. They will carry her off to slavery in the dank caves of their violent underground world.

I'm pathetic, Ophelia thinks, abandoning the clutches of her fantasy. I even dream of being carried off by trees. Too much Tolkien and not enough life! she scolds herself.

Ophelia sets up the kettle for an instant latté. Then she sorts the weeks' accumulated mail on the kitchen counter as she does every Sunday. Only one envelope looks personal. Expensive, her fingertips tell her. No return address. Mailed from New York on Memorial Day.

"I was the happiest man in the world," she reads on a crisp crease, "Now I'm the loneliest." Ophelia skips to the signature: "Chris."

Before she can read the rest, the timer on her stove beeps.

***

Ophelia sets up Loneliest Chris, freshly baked brownies, her coffee, the *Los Angeles Times*, and suntan lotion on a low table. She gets comfortable with her childhood pillow as a neck rest in a lounge chair under the trees—dawn's monsters turned shade-giving allies by the residential pool. Ophelia calls her habits and rituals "healthy priorities." One typed page from an ex-boyfriend isn't enough to shake those.

"Ophelia's got brownies!" shouts Bob, her friend and neighbor, from a balcony above her head.

"Enough to share?" A hungry smack follows the question posed in the depths of Bob's apartment.

"I'll swap them for a single straight man!" Ophelia forces a laugh. God, I sound desperate, she cringes at herself. I'm also tired of pretending that single, straight, and forty is okay.

"She's joking," says Bob. "This is LA."

Middle-aged Bob and young Flavor-of-the-Month show up in his-and-his shark-infested swimming trunks and identical mirrored sunglasses.

"I'm in the wrong place at the wrong time," Ophelia mutters, seeing herself fourfold on their hungry faces. "Unavailable hunks dig into my baking. I should be serving these to an adoring husband and two healthy kids who love me to death for taking such good care of them."

"Thanks for the plural." Bob sucks in his softening middle. "You wouldn't have time to bake if you had a husband and kids," he adds through gooey, brown teeth. "Delicious."

Pink and blue sharks run off to play in the pool. Ophelia takes a sip of coffee and gives in to the lure of the letter:

Dear Ophelia,

I'm sure you're surprised to hear from me after all this time. I saw you've kept up with the alumni newsletter—as have I.

My life took some very interesting turns since I last saw you. I went back to school and got an MBA. Since then, I've had an exceptional life right here in New York. I'm financially successful, working for a large consulting firm where I've been a partner for eight years now. I'm also on several boards and stay fit with a personal trainer. I have known complete happiness followed by a cruel loss.

His wife, Ophelia assumes, although happiness and loss are nameless. Two decades compressed onto one sheet of paper. She closes her eyes and puts Chris before her: six foot four, two hundred athletic pounds, Norwegian blue eyes.

"Who's this from?" Grinning sharks cling to Bob's wet thighs and interrupt her ruminations. He helps himself to another brownie and openly reads the entire letter.

"I've done nothing with my life!" says Ophelia. "I can't meet a decent guy! My job is a rat-race parody. Even my mother tells me I'm a loser. I've got the worst life."

"Shake it up, baby," says Flavor-of-the-Month and playfully bites Bob's shoulder. "'Menopause is *the* time to change your life.' That's what my mom says, anyway."

"I'm not *that* old!" Ophelia resents being lumped with his mother.

"That's Timmy—gorgeous and tactless," says Bob to somewhat excuse his insensitive lover. "Who's Chris?"

"Ex-boyfriend who had a full life," Ophelia reduces the page to a line.

***

Nothing personal, Ophelia decides and adds wryly, It can and will be used against you.

My life is personal, she rails against caution a moment later. If I'm going to write back at all, it's got to be—

"Think of yourself!" Her mother's voice on the telephone sounds shrill and bitter. "Why's he writing to you after all this time? Certainly not because he's interested in you!"

Ophelia already regrets that she told her mother about the letter. "Chris sounds sad."

"You were in love with him," her mother points out. "He wasn't in love with you. He lied to you. He cheated on you. That guy alone caused you more pain than all the losers you've dated since combined!"

151

"He's been through enough," Ophelia argues. "Chris doesn't need an ex-girlfriend lecturing him on the past. He needs support and understanding." Then she hangs up on her mother and pours her heart out to Chris.

***

"Life's been hard on you," Chris e-mails Ophelia a few days later.

"What does he want from you?" sniffs her mother during their regular evening chat and warns, "He's lonely, Ophelia. I remember that man—the good-looking type who flirts with everyone. Don't forget: he cheated on you and lied to you. Those kinds of flaws don't go away! They get worse!"

"I'm just corresponding with an old friend, mom. Plus, I'm in LA and he's in

New York. It's not like I'm having dinner with him."

"You make very bad choices," her mother insists. "You should be looking to marry a nice doctor, not chasing after old dreams or hanging out with gay men."

"I was unlucky," Ophelia defends who she has become—far removed from the ideal self she and her mother concocted when she was growing up.

Listening to her mother brings back memories of the sunny New York spring day when her heart broke. Ophelia and her best friend Alva strolled through Greenwich Village looking for an ice cream parlor to indulge their shared weakness for raspberry ice cream. I was who I wanted to be, Ophelia remembers her young self. I was studying art, I was in love with Chris, and I had all these dreams just waiting to come true.

153

Suddenly Alva grabbed Ophelia's arm and pointed across the street to a couple seated at a sidewalk café. "Isn't that Chris?"

It was. He wore a white shirt open at the neck, the sleeves rolled up to his elbows, and held hands with a smiling, blonde-haired woman.

"Who's the skinny blonde?" Alva pushed curvy Ophelia to cross Sixth Avenue, adding her grandmother's wisdom, "Better a horrible end than an endless horror!"

"I can't," Ophelia pleaded with Alva. "I feel too sick to talk to him right now."

"You're just going to walk away?"

Ophelia hurried back to her dorm. There, she remembers now, she spent days curled up in her bed. She had been too sick to move, eat, or even talk. After a while, her roommate prevailed and Ophelia confronted Chris.

"Hazel's just a friend," Chris said back then. "I swear. I'd never lie to you."

The same evening, friends told her they had seen Chris at the movies with a girl called Hazel. They wanted to know when Chris and Ophelia had broken up and offered their sympathies.

"Was your wife someone I knew?" Ophelia asks him in her next e-mail.

"No. I met Joan a few years after you left New York," Chris answers promptly and adds, "She was the most wonderful woman in the world."

***

"Teenage warriors armed with burning Molotov cocktails burst into a dark movie theater packed with elderly couples." The new hot talent in

155

Hollywood—stylish Oscar-winning writer/producer Ophelia—pitches the opening of a future hit sci-fi/horror/action movie to Francis Ford Coppola and Steven Spielberg over an exquisite sushi dinner at Yamashiro.

Ophelia sighs at the knock on her door and drops the fantasy before the contracts are signed. She opens the door to Bob. "I'm the only woman in LA who never tried to be in movies. I don't even have a hot script to send around."

"There's a Donkeys and Fairies Celebration down on Venice Beach. Timmy and I are heading there now. Would you like to join us?"

"Do you think I should call Chris?" she asks instead of answering his invitation.

"Absolutely not." Bob shakes his head emphatically. "Wait for him to call you. He's a guy. Let him chase you. If you call, he'll think you're chasing him. You're not chasing him, are you?"

"He won't be in," Ophelia calms her confidante. "It's Midsummer's Night, even in New York. He's probably out with friends, like everybody else—except me."

"I just asked you to join us," Bob reminds her. "Come on. If you stay in, you'll just do something stupid. I know you."

"I won't call him." She pushes Bob out the door. "Have fun, and thanks for asking, but I'm really not in the mood to be the only girl with the hormones to match the outfit."

She closes the door, waits for the rattle of the elevator, and dials Chris's number.

His voice, deeper than she remembers, requests name, date and time of call, and promises, "I'll get back to you as soon as possible." Ophelia takes a deep breath and launches into her prepared message.

"Hi, Chris, this is Ophelia. Just thought I'd call and wish you a—"

"Hi, Ophelia."

She almost drops the phone. "You screen your calls?"

"It's my business number," says Chris. "I don't usually take business calls at night."

"It's the number you gave me."

"Sorry," says Chris. "I'm glad you called, though. I've been feeling really depressed."

"I'm sorry," Ophelia stammers. "You never said when . . . "

"It's been a year and a half," says Chris. "I can say it, but I don't believe it."

"I thought you'd be out with friends."

"I rarely go out. I work more than ever. I function pretty well during the day. I hate coming home, though. I'dgo out with just about anyone not to be alone in my apartment, but then, when I'm with people, I don't even hear what they're saying. I was out with really good friends earlier. But I couldn't tell you what we talked about." He goes on and tells her about his many different circles of friends and their efforts to distract him, his personal trainer and the weights he lifts, his involvement on several boards and his contributions there, his investment strategies that have paid handsomely for himself and his clients, his hobbies and his expertise as a skier. He ends the hour-long monologue with, "Hey, I can't believe you called. I thought you might. I mean, I hoped you would."

"Well, here I am."

"I've got very special memories of you, Ophelia. We always talked—I remember that about us. Hearing your voice just now feels like we've kept in touch all these years. You sound just the same."

"That's good, I guess," she says and regrets what she wrote in her letter about her failed life. "My life hasn't been as glamorous as yours."

"I hope I haven't scared you off by telling you so much about myself and my feelings."

"I'm really sorry about your loss," says Ophelia. "It's fine to say how you're feeling, Chris. It's not good to keep feelings bottled up inside."

"I've been doing that," says Chris. "Keeping things inside. I'm not sure people want to hear it. They're used to me being the big, solid guy. Unhappy and successful don't really go together well."

"You can tell me anything at any time," Ophelia offers. "That's what old friends are for."

As soon as she hangs up, her phone rings again.

"I've been trying to get you," says Bob, sounding irritated. "Timmy lost my house keys in the sand and I need the spare. You still have my spare?"

"Sure. I'll buzz you in and have the key ready. You're not going to be late, are you?"

"No. It's not that great here. Way too many fairies, even for my liking. We're on our way back."

"Okay. See you," says Ophelia and is about to hang up.

"You called him," says Bob. "That's why I couldn't get through."

"Chris needs a friend," Ophelia defends her action. "I can be that friend. The other stuff—that was so long ago. We were just kids!"

"Your mother's going to have a fit! Didn't she tell you to stay away from him?"

"I'm not going to tell her. Besides, she told me to stay away from you, too."

***

"If you were here, I'd make us coffee," says Chris on Independence Day. His call has just interrupted Ophelia's cheer-up brunch with newly-single-and-moping Bob.

162

"I can't fly to New York right now," says Ophelia and laughs at the outrageous suggestion. "I blew my savings at Easter with my mom in Florida."

"If money's what's stopping you," says Chris, "I'll send you a ticket. It's just money, Ophelia. And I've got money."

"Or you could come here," Ophelia quickly suggests. "I'll show you the famous and infamous mansions of the rich and scandalous."

"I don't fly," says Chris after a pause.

Tell him to take the train, Bob writes on a pad, eavesdropping shamelessly. Ophelia shakes her head and is about to speak when Bob takes the phone from her hand and covers the transmitter.

"Meet on your own turf," Bob insists. "If you're not smart enough to stay away from this guy, at least play it safe!"

Ophelia retrieves her phone, runs to her bedroom, and closes the door on Bob's hurt face.

"I can't believe you stopped painting!" Chris changes the subject. "You were determined to be a famous artist, Ophelia."

"I haven't held a brush in years," she confesses and gets comfortable on her bed. "Nobody bought my pieces. I wasn't good enough to go professional. I've been working in a furniture store the last ten years. Sometimes I get to put people's houses together. That's artistic, in a way."

"You should give it another try," says Chris. "You've got it in you to be really great! You just need a chance. You've got talent. I know because I've had a lot to do with artists over the years. And I'm a very good art critic."

"Aren't you in finance now? Anyway, it was kind of tough being creative when I was working two jobs to pay the rent."

"That's what I mean!" his excited voice travels from New York to LA. "You should make the time. Give yourself a chance!"

"Do you still pour your coffee from one cup into another to cool it?"

Their first breakfast together dances on her ceiling. Chris cracked and whipped eggs and poured them into a sizzling pan. She wore one of his T-shirts and danced to "Can't Buy Me Love" playing on the radio. Butter melted on hot toast as he kissed her. Then he poured the coffee. It was too hot, so he took another cup, chilled it with ice cubes, and transferred the hot coffee into the cold cup. They shared a coffee-flavored kiss.

Bob knocks on the bedroom door.

"You remember all that?"

"Like your jeans." She smiles as she says this and throws a pillow at Bob, who sticks his head around the door. "You're the only man I ever met who has his jeans dry-cleaned and pressed with a crease."

Bob falls to his knees and clutches his chest in mock distress.

"You really cared about me," says Chris.

"I was madly in love with you," declares Ophelia from the distance of twenty years and the other coast. Slumped on the floor, Bob begs her to shut up.

***

Ophelia comes home after a long day moving furniture around the showroom to a huge parcel with sketch pads and pencils, inks and watercolors, oils and canvases, and a note:

I went to the best shop in the Village and had them put it together. I want you to have the best of everything when you make your dream come true.

Love,

Chris

"My work could be bad," says Ophelia after she has thanked Chris profusely.

"Never," Chris sounds absolutely convinced. "You're an artist. You're also a passionate woman. Passion's what art is about! I wish I could do it. I can't even draw stick figures. I take excellent photographs—but you remember that. I'm also fairly good at writing about art, as

167

you know. Besides, I've got a lot of contacts in the field, Ophelia. As soon as you've got some pieces together, send them to me and I'll help you get an exhibit here in New York."

"You'd do that for me?" Ophelia stares in panic at the white canvases now piled on her dining table.

Chris encourages Ophelia to develop a portfolio of sketches, watercolors, and even oils and then lets her go to get started.

Ophelia promptly calls Bob and invites him to come over and see the surprise.

"He certainly spent money," says Bob after he has inspected the gift. "What does he expect in return?"

"He wants me to paint," says Ophelia and hugs Bob. "Don't sound like my mom. Be happy for me, Bob."

***

"Exciting exhibit by LA-based artist Ophelia (first name only!). In 'Before Words,' present-day impressions of LA's grim reality challenge fantastic creatures. 'Real days and the dream-helpers who get us through them,' states the artist in the program notes. We agree with Ophelia's claim: 'Life's richer with dreams.' At Village Master's Gallery, now through the end of the month. Not to be missed."

"I've spent the last three hours looking at your work," Chris interrupts Ophelia's Labor Day dream. "I really like the strong blacks and blues. I think it's great you've done a series. Some really interesting details, Ophelia."

"Wow. Thanks. I'm glad you like them. I wasn't sure if you would. I mean, it's been years since I last held a brush."

"You were always excellent with detail," Chris continues. "What exactly is the theme you're going for?"

"Before words." Ophelia takes a breath as she tries to formulate the emotions she captured in her work. "It's the moment between when I see something—something out of the corner of my eye, or when it is not quite in focus, or when it is oddly lit by sunrise or sunset and the shapes are not quite clear, or when I wish to see something that isn't there, or isn't there but could be—and when I try to put that image into words."

There is a long silence as Ophelia catches her breath and waits for Chris to speak.

"Interesting," says Chris finally. "You need to be in New York, Ophelia. You need to be where the galleries are. You've got to paint and work at it full-time. Give it your all."

"I did," says Ophelia and feels her hands growing cold. "I gave it my all. I worked every day after work and on Sundays. My boss already wanted to know why I wasn't doing any overtime anymore. It's all the time I have. It's got to be enough, Chris. I told you that a few weeks ago. That's why I stopped—before. There are just so many hours in a day—"

"I want you to keep trying," Chris insists. "You said in your first letter that you've failed all your dreams. It doesn't have to be that way! I know I failed you back then. I was young and stupid and just didn't get how lucky I was to have a beautiful girl like you love me. But life's taught me a few lessons, Ophelia. There are many things I can't control, but I can be a friend. I can encourage you. I can maybe even help you have at least one of your dreams come true."

"Why?"

"Because," he clears his throat before he continues, "I was in love with you, too."

"If you were, why did you see other women?"

"I guess I wanted it all," says Chris. "But I've learned from my mistakes. That's one thing that's definitely true about me: I'm always willing to learn. I'm always trying to be a better person. I don't make the same mistake twice."

"What happened to the other girl?" Ophelia bites her lip as she waits for his answer.

"Hazel's been out of my life for decades, Ophy." He uses the nickname he had given her. "It took a while for me to get what I had done. I was young and cocky and had a bit of growing up to do. But that was a very long time ago. I'm nothing like that anymore."

"You never admitted cheating on me."

"I've regretted what I did to you then for the last twenty years of my life, Ophy. If I could do it over, I would," says Chris. "I want to be everything for you. I can be your most helpful critic, president of your fan club, and your very best friend. Whatever you need."

"I'm looking for my soul mate," says Ophelia, her pulse still racing from his admission that he had been in love with her.

"It's hell being alone," says Chris. "But now that we're talking again, I don't feel so alone. I'm honored that you sent me your work."

"It's just a beginning," says Ophelia.

"Yes, absolutely," Chris laughs. "It will get better and better. I just know it. I have complete faith in your talent."

"Okay!"

"Okay. Get to work, little artist," says Chris.

After they hang up, Ophelia calls Bob.

"Chris is lonely in New York and I'm lonely in LA."

"It's also safe," Bob points out. "You've got this great thing going on the phone. Keep it that way."

***

"I'm in love!" Ophelia's mistress-of-gore wig glows in the candlelight. "I've fallen in love on the phone. I know I'm taking a chance. My boss thinks I'm nuts. My mom thinks I'm nuts."

"Did he invite you?" Bob adjusts the tail on his red devil leotard.

"No," Ophelia admits to the little twist in her plan. "It's a surprise."

"You can always stay in a hotel if things don't work out." Bob eyes a nimble cherub checking out the offerings on the buffet. "Turn visiting a prospective lover into a cultural vacation."

"I'm really in love." Ophelia returns a skull-shaped muffin and takes a plain celery stick. "I must be—I've lost five pounds."

The cherub asks Bob to dance, and they disappear in the white cloud that covers the dance floor.

***

She places her childhood pillow behind her head and imagines Chris meeting her at the airport. He's holding a gigantic bouquet of red roses, she leaps into his arms, and finally they kiss. It will be the kiss to beat all kisses. A kiss that will go on and on. Breathless. A kiss they've been teasing each other with for weeks.

The flight is long and bumpy. She catches up on fashion magazines and watches the only romantic in-flight movie available. Finally, the plane prepares for landing and excitement replaces the tedium of the flight. Ophelia checks her appearance in a small makeup mirror, runs a comb through her hair, and straightens her rumpled clothing. Then, as the plane descends, she looks with delight at the spectacle of New York by night. My new home, she thinks. My ex- and future home, if things work out, she corrects. She stuffs the old pillow into her large carry-on and tries to contain her impatience as she shuffles behind other passengers dragging their luggage off the plane.

Ophelia pushes through the slow-moving throng following the arrows to arrivals and baggage claim. From the top of the escalator, she scans the hall. Men in dark suits hold up name signs, and groups wave and shout at arriving friends and family. She concentrates on the faces that are rapidly coming closer as the escalator reaches ground level and is disappointed not to see Chris. He's probably waiting for me at baggage claim, she thinks. It would make sense. She scans the area, certain that at six foot four, Chris will be easy to spot.

Disappointed again, Ophelia takes a cart, piles her carry-ons in the basket, and heads to the belt for the flight from LAX. Hundreds of people soon flock to the same belt. All, as far as she can see, under six foot four.

Ophelia finally spots her suitcase, lifts it onto her cart, and looks for a quiet area to call Chris. She pushes the cart to a remote seating area behind tall pillars and sees a man with sunglasses obscuring his face get to his feet as she approaches.

"Hi, Ophelia," says the man, who is definitely tall, albeit twice the width she remembers.

"Were you hiding in case I look awful?" asks Ophelia and swallows her disappointment.

"You look the same," says Chris. His wedding band and Rolex watch reflect the neon lighting of the arrival hall as he lifts her suitcases from the pushcart. "I'm sorry. No. Of course not. There were just so many people. I'm not good in crowds. Anyway, my Benz is in parking."

"Can you see with those in the dark?" wonders Ophelia, pointing at the gold-rimmed sunglasses.

He blushes and removes them. "I recognized you immediately," says Chris. "I always liked the way you looked. I've put on a bit of weight since you last saw me."

As she follows him to his gleaming car, she wonders what exercises he did with his trainer.

Ophelia recalls his baby blue Beetle as he plays with the controls of the fully automatic adult toy. I used to put my hand on his when he shifted gears, Ophelia thinks, and smiles at the memory.

They head for New York City. Instead of the rock music she had expected, Chris tunes in to the Bloomberg report. She looks over at the ringed hand gripping the steering wheel. When did he get so rigid? she wonders, recalling his easy handling of the old car, one hand always free to shift gears, touch her knee, or play with her hair. We kissed in the Lincoln Tunnel, Ophelia continues her reverie as they approach the city.

"Fucking stock market!" Chris ex - plodes. "Thank God I've moved most of my money into bonds."

"I never had enough cash to care one way or another," Ophelia interrupts his expletive-riddled rant about NASDAQ, the DOW, and other metrics. "Is this what you do at work?"

"My wife and I followed the market closely," Chris explains. "It was just one of those things we did. I'm in a different branch of finance. Thank God. Those guys are jumping out of windows with the shit that's going on."

Ophelia nods. She has heard of the crisis and what it is doing to New York.

"Remember?" asks Chris, gliding through E-Z Pass at the tunnel. "We couldn't keep our hands off each other."

"What if it's not the same?" says Ophelia and tries to find a memory of him desiring her.

"You were really crazy about that man—but that was twenty years ago!" her mother had said when Ophelia confessed her plan to visit Chris for Thanksgiving.

Ophelia's mouth is dry. I don't know the man driving this flashy car, she realizes. He's a stranger. I've just flown six hours for a blind date!

"You want adventure," Bob said when she told him. "Crossing the country to stay with a complete stranger is about as adventurous and irresponsible as it gets!"

"Only one way to find out," says Chris. There's a thin film of perspiration on his upper lip as he adds, "I was certainly surprised when I got your call this morning."

"Isn't that what you wanted?" Ophelia thinks of their conversations, many invitations, and his sadness at his loneliness. "I thought you'd be happy."

"Sorry, that came out wrong. I'm thrilled you're here. I've always wanted us to be together, Ophy." He speeds across town to Fifth Avenue and adds, "I hated the way we broke up back then."

"Nobody leaves me!" young Chris shouted back then. "I didn't lie. I love you, Ophy. We're made to be together," he said repeatedly. Then he called and asked for one more chance. He sent letters swearing he was faithful. She suddenly also remembers Chris waiting for her outside her dorm.

"I want to kill you," he said, his breath already a putrid, alcoholic weapon.

"Then do it quickly," Ophelia remembers saying. I forgot that, Ophelia realizes, and fear spreads from her stomach to her fingers.

"I made a huge mistake back then," says Chris and reaches for her hand. "But I'm not like that anymore, Ophy. I've changed. You'll see."

"I forgot how cold New York is in the winter," says Ophelia to explain her icy fingers. "I used to come back for Christmas until my mom moved to Florida. But that's more than ten years now."

"Here we are." He drops her hand as he pulls up in front of a well-lit entrance. "My building's the best run in the city.

Actually, it was a wreck until I became president of the board." White-gloved doormen respectfully greet Chris, pile her cases onto a cart, and valet the car.

"My terrace has a great view," says Chris as the elevator moves swiftly to his floor. He tips the doorman who deposits her luggage in the white-on-white entrance.

"People just love my apartment when they see it," Chris says once the door is closed. To Ophelia, he sounds like a little boy hoping for her approval. "I'll give you a tour. I hope you'll like it too, but if there's anything you don't like, we'll just change it." He laughs and then leads her over white marble floors through the living room into a dark back room.

"This is the second bedroom I had turned into a study," he says.

Ophelia stops his hand from turning on the light and wraps her arms tightly around his neck. "Hi, Chris," she says and finally kisses her first love.

"You'll have the dreams you wrote about in your letter." Chris raises his head after their lips touch briefly but holds her in his arms in the dark room. "I always thought of you as a great artist."

"You dropped photography and went into business." Ophelia hides her disappointment at the brevity of the kiss and leans into the embrace.

"We were into careers. There wasn't much of a career in photography." Chris releases her, turns on a desktop lamp, and shakes the watch on his wrist.

Ophelia touches his back. "I remember sinking into you," she says and waits for her hand to get to know him—the soft back, the thick waist, the heavy

185

neck and jowls. "I didn't wake up from that altered state until I saw you holding hands with—"

"I'm not like that anymore," Chris interrupts. "This time, it'll be perfect, Ophy. Just wait and see."

History, biographies, ethics, business—hard-cover books only, alphabetized and dust-free—rise from floor to ceiling on opposite walls of the room, interrupted by a few rows of books on painters.

"You don't read fiction anymore?" she asks him.

"They're Joan's," he says.

"And you gave up on the Knicks?" Ophelia points at a framed picture of the Dodgers above the built-in writing desk.

"That's Joan's team," he says and pulls Ophelia from the study to the adjoining bedroom. "Come, I'm sure you want to unpack."

***

The welcoming committee stands in silver frames on a long dresser. In the first row are three little girls with Chris's eyes. "My nieces," says Chris, setting down Ophelia's luggage. "And that's my brother and his wife. The one with the long dark hair is my sister with her husband, and the frame behind shows my in-laws. And that's Joan." He flushes and then turns quickly to a smiling peroxide blonde on the nightstand. "That's my favorite picture of my mom."

"Which side do you sleep on?"

Chris nods to the other side of the bed, and the telephone rings as if on cue. He excuses himself, goes to his study, and closes the door.

"Who are you?" the little girls in matching dresses climb from their frames and sit on the bed.

"She's Uncle Chris's old girlfriend," their mother informs them.

"How long are you staying?" the children want to know.

"So, what do you do?" ask the men before she can answer the girls.

"I paint," says Ophelia aloud.

Chris wants me here, she reminds herself and escorts the girls back to their elegant frame. I'm letting my imagination get the better of me. It's normal that he's got these pictures lined up. This is his home. She unzips her suitcase, grabs a neat pile of blouses, and opens the bifold door to the walk-in closet.

A long row of handbags, hat boxes piled to the ceiling, square stacks of silk scarves, sweaters in plastic cases, and shirts folded to envelope perfection fill the shelves. Rows of jackets with matching skirts and trousers, summer and winter dresses, and terry cloth bathrobes on pink padded hangers occupy every remaining inch of space. Ophelia closes the door and drops her blouses back in the suitcase. She takes her old pillow from her bag and hugs it to her chest.

"What's that?" asks Chris when he returns.

"My old pillow," says Ophelia. "I've slept on it since I was five."

"That's what it looks like," says Chris and raises his eyebrows. "You won't need that. I've got excellent pillows and a very expensive duvet on my bed."

"Is there a place I can put my things?"

"I've emptied this drawer for you," he says and opens one of a dozen under

Joan's gaze. "I can also give you some hangers if you need them. Come, I'll show you the guest bathroom."

Ophelia takes her vanity and follows him to an elegant gray-on-gray, marble-tiled space. "Mine is on the other side. I'll leave you to freshen up. I've got champagne for us."

An old, silver hairbrush and comb and silver plates with small trinkets and souvenirs neatly arranged next to the deep sink chill Ophelia. This was his wife's, she realizes. And he hasn't touched it since she died. She tucks her case in the small space between the vanity and the bathtub and splashes cold water on her face.

***

"You're the sexiest woman I know," says Chris when she joins him in his discreetly dimmed living room. "I always loved that about you."

"What did you love about me?" Ophelia accepts a glass of champagne. She looks for a comfortable chair among the straight-backed white decor.

"You have this effect on me," says Chris. He sets their glasses down on white leather coasters and takes her in his arms. "You turn me on like no other woman, Ophy. Come, be nice. Come and play."

Ophelia stares past his shoulder and out the window as he bends and undresses her. Chris cups her breasts as she imagines her dreams slipping down the façade to Washington Square and disappearing in a Village gutter.

"We'll have a great time," says Chris caressing her. "I want to help you become the success you should be, Ophy." He finally kisses Ophelia, kisses her deeply, kisses her until she can no longer tell where her mouth begins. And just as suddenly as his mouth took possession of hers, he lifts his head and declares: "LA isn't right for you. You're an East Coast woman. You'll paint and be successful—here in New York where it counts!"

***

Ophelia returns to the bathroom and stares at her flushed face. Sex, she realizes. It's what we had then, too. I forgot how much Chris likes sex. And I'm in love, just as I was then!

"Here you are!" Chris stands in the door with a wrapped parcel in his hands. "I'm waiting for you in the living room. Come. I've refilled our glasses, and there's shrimp cocktail."

He kisses her tenderly on the cheek. "Happy?"

Ophelia nods. "I am a bit hungry. The food on the plane wasn't very good."

"I bet," Chris laughs. "I can certainly do better."

He surprises her with keys to his car and apartment.

"I want to take excellent care of you." He folds the discarded wrapping paper. "Everything that's mine is yours, Ophy. I want to share everything with you. And you can paint all day. But at night, I need you to have time for me! We'll go to movies, the theater, restaurants . . . if we ever get out of bed, that is."

She listens to him speak about his successes, saving businesses with his creative ideas and sensible approach, over a chilled shrimp starter. She tries to track the different committees he chairs as baked sea bass with creamed spinach and mashed potatoes is delivered piping hot from a nearby restaurant. She decides not to mention the obvious ineffectiveness of his personal trainer as they finish off the meal with runny Camembert and soft baguette. Then Chris again escorts Ophelia to the stone-tiled bathroom.

"Don't be too long," he says and caresses her hips. "I can't wait to sleep with you in my arms."

My eyes are shining, she notices in the mirror above the sink. I'm in love.

Lightly perfumed and glowing, she comes into the bedroom as Chris puts Joan's photograph away in the top drawer of his nightstand.

"Can't have sex with her watching," he mutters and frowns as Ophelia replaces his pillows with her old one.

"It's what I'm used to," she explains.

"As long as it's not on during the day," Chris concedes. "I like a nicely made bed."

***

"How about a kiss?" Chris says, freshly showered and shaved.

"You don't eat breakfast?"

"Never at home. This is New York," he laughs. "Best coffee's on the streets! And it's just fifty cents!" He kisses her and pinches her thighs. "Just making sure you think about me all day!" he says and leaves.

Ophelia unpacks her sketch pad and pencils and takes them to his study. She plans to surprise Chris with a new piece. However, Chris's computer and fax machine, the printer, and stacks of folders cover the working desk and every other surface

The first hallway door is a shoe closet—Chris and Joan's footwear from floor to ceiling, arranged by color and heel height, with polished boots separated from assorted sneakers, separated from sling-back sandals, separated from business blue and brown and black pumps, separated from sensible loafers—the lot. The next two closets are packed with coats, jackets, and wraps, sorted by occasion and season.

"I won't cry," she tells Bob, whom she wakes with her call. "And I'm not telling my mom! She'd have a fit! He's gone to work—too busy to take a few days off to be with me. I guess that's my fault for surprising him. And there's just no room for me, you know?"

Her phone to her ear, she walks into the bathroom, slides the mirrored medicine-cabinet door, and describes what she sees to her confidante on the other coast. "Hairpins in a dusty glass jar, medicated mouthwash, anti-wrinkle body cream—yup, it's expired. Toothpaste, conditioner, shampoo, tweezers, scissors, nail files, and sun protection—also expired. I feel like I'm invading. Joan passed away almost two years ago, and it's like he's waiting for her to come home."

"He's still in mourning," says Bob. "I'm no expert, Ophelia, but you might want to let him know how you feel. Let the guy know you need some room for your stuff. In a nice way. He told you he wants you there, right?"

"Yes."

"Give him a chance."

Ophelia thanks Bob for listening to her fears and hangs up. She sees the bed has been made and looks for her pillow.

She looks in the closet and under the bed. She looks in her suitcases. She opens every closet and every drawer. She finally gets a stepladder from the kitchen and finds her pillow on the top shelf, behind bags and hat boxes, in the walk-in closet.

She discovers coffee beans and raspberry jam in the fridge and a collection of coffeepots, espresso machines, coffee cups, and mugs of all sizes in the cupboards. She makes herself a pot of coffee and decides to use the glass-topped dining table to work.

***

Ten silent hours later, Ophelia welcomes Chris with a sloppy kiss.

"I really missed you," he says between kisses. "I thought about you all day long. I kept remembering last night. What a distraction." He releases her and loosens his tie. "How was your first day back in New York?"

"Really quiet," says Ophelia. "Your phones didn't ring once!"

"I have the calls forwarded to my office," he explains and heads to the kitchen. "I didn't want you to be disturbed."

"I don't mind taking messages for you."

"I don't want you to. You're not my secretary, Ophy."

"This total silence is spooky."

"There's an amazing hi-fi stereo system in the study," says Chris as he pours himself a beer. "You could listen to music." He runs water into the sink and squirts detergent over her used mugs. Then he sees her sketch pad and pencils on the dining room table and grabs handy wipes and Windex.

"No one's ever used this table. I mean—if anything had dropped on the chairs! They're real leather!"

"I'm sorry," stammers Ophelia. "There's no room in the study, Chris. This was the only available surface. I'm also not sure where you would want me to set up my easel and paints if I were to live here."

Chris stops cleaning. He looks around his living room and then sighs. "You'll have to be out tomorrow anyway."

"Why?"

"The housekeeper's coming."

"I won't be in her way," says Ophelia. "She does one room at a time, right?"

"She cleans at my in-laws', and I'm not ready for them to know about you. I mean, I want to be the one to tell them about us. I don't want them to hear about you from the housekeeper. That just wouldn't be good."

"So . . . where do you want me to go?"

"There's the Metropolitan and the Guggenheim," he promptly suggests and then smiles. "That's not a bad place for an artist to spend her morning, is it?"

"I could meet some of the gallerists you know," Ophelia suggests. "I'd like to get a sense of what kind of work they represent." She looks at Chris expectantly.

"I'll have to do some research," he finally says.

"What research?"

"Just a couple of calls. You know— see who knows who."

"You don't know anybody? I thought you said—"

"I said I'd help when you're ready, Ophy. You're coming along. I can see how much effort you're putting into it."

"Effort . . . what do you mean?" asks Ophelia. "My work is original but not inaccessible. Who are you thinking about?"

"I can't say off the top of my head."

"Well, just give me some art shows you've been to," she prompts.

"It doesn't mean anything which art shows I've been to. I still know good art when I see it!" He brushes away her doubts regarding his expertise. "Look, if you don't think my advice is valid, I'll show your work to a friend. She's in the field and I trust her opinion.

"When?"

"After the holidays. I can't really impose on anyone over Thanksgiving. Come, grab a coat and let's go out to dinner," says Chris, changing the subject. "I'm starving!"

They take the elevator down and cross the lobby, nod at the doorman, and step out into the cold and windy street. Ophelia reaches for Chris's hand.

"Not here!" He yanks his hand away. "Someone could see us."

"So?" Ophelia feels her throat constrict.

"I told you, Ophy," Chris frowns and shakes his head at her. "I'm a very private person. I've never been one for public display of affection."

"It's not like I'm pawing you," Ophelia laughs at him. "This is New York, Chris. Nobody cares!"

"I care," says Chris and blushes. "Plus, we could run into people I know. I'm not ready for that."

"Okay. I'm sorry," Ophelia apologizes.

Later, Ophelia brushes her teeth in Joan's bathroom, throws her dirty clothes into Joan's hamper, and joins Chris in Joan's bed. She closes her eyes and tries to ignore the knowing grins on the men's faces as Chris pushes up her nightshirt. She wants to apologize to the embarrassed mothers who yank Chris's giggling nieces from the picture frame as he pins her onto the mattress.

"I'm madly in love with you," Chris murmurs, rolls back to his side, and falls asleep.

***

"The damned museum doesn't open until ten!" Ophelia wakes Bob in LA.

"What time is it?" yawns Bob.

"It's eight thirty." Ophelia suddenly feels guilty. "I'm sorry, Bob. I keep forgetting you're three hours behind."

"I'm up now," says Bob. "Why are you in front of a museum at eight thirty?"

"So the housekeeper doesn't see me."

"The what?"

"I'm sorry. I shouldn't unload all this on you." Ophelia crosses Fifth Avenue in search of a coffee shop. Bob on the other end offers his attention, and she shares the last twenty-four hours with him.

"How's the sex?"

"That's good," admits Ophelia. "There's plenty of that."

"Give the rest of the stuff time," advises Bob. "My relationships end when the sex isn't fun anymore. Either that or they get too clingy, or I get too clingy. Play

205

it cool; you've only been with the guy for two days."

Then Ophelia breaks down and tells Bob that Chris has no contacts in the art field.

"I don't understand," sobs Ophelia on the phone to Bob. "Why did he say I should paint again? Why did he say he'd help?"

"It's what you wanted to hear," Bob responds knowingly.

***

Ophelia returns to a cleaned apartment in the afternoon. She brews a pot of coffee and decides to check the bookcases for something fun to read. The art books catch her eye. She picks the playful surrealist Dali from the shelf and opens the cover.

"From Hazelnut to Chris-squirrel, 'A love that flies high!' Christmas 1994." The dedication inside the front cover hits Ophelia like a fist.

"From Hazelnut to Chris-squirrel, 'We continue living our love like perfect works of art!' Christmas 2000," in Monet.

"From Hazelnut to Chris-squirrel, 'Rainbows of tender colors unite us forever.' Christmas 2010," in Chagall.

Ophelia finds romantic Christmas dedications in every art book from 1994 to the present, without interruption, when Boucher appeared in the collection: "To celebrate a love that has overcome all odds."

"My mother was right: flaws don't go away," Ophelia tells Bob.

"You must get to the bottom of this!" says Bob. "It doesn't sound good, but there might be a simple explanation."

Ophelia lets Bob go and sits down at Chris's precious dining table, careful not to drop any coffee on the white leather chair.

It is late when she hears the door open.

"Ophy, you here?" Chris calls and turns on the light.

"I'm here," she manages.

"Why are you in the dark?" Chris bends and kisses her cheek. "Everything okay?"

"I've been thinking about Hazel," Ophelia admits. "About you and Hazel and what role she's playing in your life."

"I think she's married," Chris says. "I told you. She left my life when I met Joan."

Ophelia brings the Boucher from the study, drops it on the table, and flips the cover to the dedication.

"I can't remember when she gave me that," says Chris. "We're just friends."

"That's from last Christmas. How could you forget? There's one for every year."

"It doesn't matter," says Chris. He closes the book. "You're the only woman who matters, Ophy. You're being really stupid!"

"You said she left your life!"

"She did," shouts Chris. "We're just friends. Don't you have friends?"

"They don't write love declarations!"

"What do you think?" says Chris, and his face turns an ugly shade of red. "I was faithful to Joan! I can't help it if people love me. I can't believe you're this jealous! You know that I'm in love with you, Ophy. I know I did some pretty stupid things twenty years ago, but that's not who I am now. I'm the loyal type, Ophy."

"This is a failure." Ophelia shakes her head at him and steps back.

"What are you talking about?" Chris follows her.

"You don't know any galleries where I could show my work, do you? I have no friends here. And I'm not at home here, Chris. This whole place is still waiting for Joan to come back. You're waiting for her to come back. All you want with me is sex."

"If you loved me, you'd understand," says Chris. "I'm trying, Ophy. I'm trying really hard. I never said I knew any galleries! And I don't need to listen to you call me a liar! I'm a very successful man. I've given you everything. If it's not enough—fuck you! I can have any woman I want."

He leaves her in the living room and slams the door to the bedroom. Ophelia retrieves her old pillow from its new exile in the linen closet and settles down to a night on the straight-backed white living room sofa.

I'm an aging princess waiting to be rescued from the mess I've made of my life! she admits to herself. I really want Chris to be that knight. I want him to be my first love and my last. But there's no room for me in his castle. Every closet, cabinet, coat hook, shelf, and drawer is still stuffed with Joan's things. There must be fifty drawers in this place. I've got one! I'll talk to him, she decides. Tomorrow morning, when we've both cooled down.

Ophelia sleeps in fits, worried that she's losing her last chance at happiness. By morning, her resolve to speak with

Chris has weakened, and she decides to write him a letter instead. An honest letter, she vows. Loving but also honest. Words he can't mishear. Sentences he won't interrupt.

She goes into the empty study and sits down at his computer. The machine is on, and a folder titled "Love" is open. Ophelia sees her name and clicks on it.

Ophelia scrolls down and sees all their correspondence from the first letter on Memorial Day to the last e-mail finalizing her travel itinerary. She feels a surge of love for Chris and shame at her own doubts. While she pouted on the living room sofa and planned all the cold and mean things she wanted to say to him, he spent the night rereading their romantic correspondence. Ophelia closes the folder and bites her lips. Should she run to him, obviously still asleep in the bedroom next door, and kiss and make up? Should she add a love note to the folder for him to find upon waking?

Ophelia reopens the "Love" folder to find their last exchange. Her eyes widen as she sees that "Ophelia" is only one of several sub-folders—at the bottom of a list that starts with "Fiona." A few increasingly devastating minutes later, Ophelia knows that her cherished Memorial Day letter went out to eight other ex-girlfriends.

Ophelia is reminded of how she felt twenty years earlier when she saw Chris with another woman. Now she sees him with eight other women. Fiona and Georgia responded politely but made it clear that Chris was not wanted in their lives. Janice, a part-time secretary, is married and had "fond memories of trips to Montauk" with Chris in her youth. She set dates to meet again. She also agreed to review Ophelia's work.

There was also Mary, who had children but was "occasionally free for a tender afternoon in the city." And the eternally-present Hazel, whom he had seen at Christmas, and who wrote most recently: "She had no talent then and has none now. Why do you waste your time? You spoil the stupid woman. Did she even like the supplies we picked out for her?"

Ophelia crawls away from the computer just as Chris strides fully dressed into the study.

"You've no idea how much you hurt me with the things you said last night," he says. "I do everything I know to help you. I'm there for you. I encourage you in every way. I'm giving you the chance nobody else would give you. You must know by now that nobody will ever love you as I do.

That's what I have to say. I'm going to have Thanksgiving dinner with Joan's family now. That was planned long before your surprise visit, and I just can't hurt their feelings. Maybe we can talk later, Ophy, and you can explain to me what it is you think I've done to you." The apartment door closes behind him.

Ophelia staggers from the study to the bathroom and is violently ill. This can't be happening to me, she thinks. This is just some horrible nightmare. She takes a hot shower, and as she reaches for the towel, she catches sight of Joan's silver hairbrush and the silver plate with trinkets that are not her own souvenirs. Instantly, the folders, the eight other women, and Chris's parting words suffocate Ophelia. She lies down on the moist bathroom floor and waits for the waves of nausea to subside.

After a while, her breathing becomes normal. She gets dressed and says good-bye to Chris's brothers and sisters, in-laws, and nieces, as well as to his mother, who smiles from her framed position on what was unofficially Ophelia's night-stand. Finally, she rescues Joan from the drawer.

"Did you know about Janice and Hazel?" Ophelia asks the photograph. "How could you stand it?"

Ophelia again wakes Bob in LA. "I'm going to find a flight to Florida. I'll stay with my mom for a few days. I know she'll say she told me so, but it beats being alone on Thanksgiving!"

***

"I woke up Thanksgiving morning," says Ophelia to Bob a few days later, "and the pillow under my head was the only thing in his apartment that felt real and safe."

They sit by the pool, sipping lattés and munching on late-night-therapy baked cookies. "It all just kind of came together," Ophelia says. "Living out of suitcases, the lie about art connections, hiding me from his family. I thought that at least his loneliness was real. But even that was a lie.

"I wanted it to work. I wanted to be in his arms at night and by his side during the day. I got half."

"Is half better than nothing?"

"No," says Ophelia. "It's worse."

Johanna Miklós

In Closing

Johanna Miklós—a new "Indie Author" — thanks the generous and talented people it took to get these stories together as a published collection (either downloaded or printed): Simona Doxan, Russell Bittner, Helga Schier, and Amy Maddox as well as the countless geniuses responsible for the world wide web, electronic devices, and print on demand technology.

These five stories cover thirty years of writing. "Breadcrumbs" and "Eugene & Kuki" were written in the 1980's; "Ophelia Rekindled" was written between 2003 and 2007; "Perfectly Pretty" and "Magariah's Flaw" are more recent.

Many more stories have appeared in print and online and a list with links can be found at the website jmiklosdotcom.